The Other Side
of
the Veil

The Other Side of the Veil

WRITTEN BY

ALAN W. HARRIS

Fruitful Tree Publishing
Luray, Virginia 22835

This book is published by:

Fruitful Tree Publishing

321 Camelot Court

Luray, Virginia 22835

www.StoriesChangeHearts.com

This book is lovingly dedicated to my best friend,
greatest supporter, and the most wonderful wife God
could have ever given me,

Valerie M. Harris,

without whom I would not be the man I am, and none
of my books would have ever been published.

*"Thank you, Sweetheart! I love you
with all of my being!"*

CONTENTS

PREFACE

A number of years ago, a very dear friend of mine named Bill and his wife came to watch several of us play a church league softball game. One of our players was late, and we were going to have to forfeit the game if we didn't start on time. Our captain scheduled our late player to bat last, and we started the game. As it turned out, our guys were doing great. It was clear that our late player was going to have to bat, but he still hadn't showed up.

In order not to forfeit the game, we needed a temporary replacement for him. The captain went over to Bill, who was well into his 70's, and asked if he would stand in for our missing player.

All he asked Bill to do was stand at the plate for four pitches. If the ump called three strikes, that would be fine, and if he walked Bill that would be fine too. We would simply put a pinch runner on for him.

With a smile Bill hobbled out of the stands, picked up a bat, and strolled up to the plate. "You don't have to do anything, Bill!" the captain called. "Just stand there for four pitches."

The first pitch was lobbed right across the plate, and Bill clobbered it! Then to all of our horror, we watched this old man SPRINT to first base with a huge grin on his face!

A runner was quickly substituted for Bill, and we all got a big laugh out of it. But sometime in the middle of the game, Bill started hurting and asked his wife to drive him home. About two in the morning, Bill was in such intense pain that his wife called an ambulance and he was rushed to the hospital. When several of the doctors consulted together, they decided that Bill had an aneurism in his aorta. The huge main artery that carries blood from his heart was swelling up like a balloon and could burst at any moment. The chief anesthesiologist in the hospital, who happened to be a friend of Bill's, had heard the emergency call and rushed down to see if he could help in this very delicate surgical procedure. He was shocked to discover that it was his good friend who was fighting for his life.

As the surgeons were discussing the best way to handle the dangerous procedure, the anesthesiologist suddenly noticed that Bill's blood pressure monitor dropped to zero. He realized Bill's aneurism had just burst. "CUT HIM!" he yelled at the surgeons. "CUT HIM NOW!"

"But he's not under anesthesia!" the surgeon shot back!"

"CUT HIM NOW, OR HE'S DEAD!" came the direct answer.

And so with no anesthesia, they began a surgery that would take hours to complete and take Bill months to recover from, but his life was saved.

When Bill was well enough to return home, I went by to see him. During our conversation, he told me an amazing story.

Bill said that as the doctors began the surgery, he found himself floating over the operating table. He watched curiously as the doctors worked furiously to save his life. Bill mentioned seeing a silver cord passing from his body on the table and extending up to his spirit where he hovered overhead. He was fascinated and listened to what the doctors were saying.

As he watched, Bill said that suddenly everything changed, and he discovered that he was walking along a garden path. Everything was beautiful, fresh, and bright. He eventually came to an ivy-covered wall with a door in it and knocked. He suddenly heard the most beautiful voice he had ever experienced asking him to choose whether to come in or return to earth.

Bill said, "Lord, I want to come in!"

"It's not time yet, Bill," the voice returned. "I want you to go back. I have more for you to do."

When Bill agreed, he woke up in pain in the ICU recovery room of the hospital.

That near-death experience meant the world to Bill. He would tear up whenever he talked about it, and from then on he was anxious to get to heaven, having no fear of death.

Bill's experience was my inspiration for writing <u>The Other Side of the Veil</u>. It seemed to me that, since God has allowed a number of people to have experiences similar to Bill's, He wants us to consider these things and learn what we can from them.

I wish to express a sincere thank you to David Morton, Michael Brown, and Becky Wilson for their valuable suggestions and biblical advice they gave to me in making this work more readable and clear.

I hope that this book is more than just an entertaining story. It is my desire that, as we consider what is on the other side of the veil, we will discover the truths God wants us to put into practice in our lives on this side of it.

Alan W. Harris

Luray, Virginia
August 6, 2022

Chapter One

"Pump that jack handle one more time, Milton."

"How about that?"

"Too much. Turn the release knob and bring it down slightly…Hold it! That's perfect! Now bring me that large crescent."

Thirty-year-old Milton Collins, who was working the jack, reached into the top tray of the rolling red tool cart and grabbed the asked for wrench. He stepped over and handed it to his partner.

"Thanks," Scott Jones said with a smile. "Now could you put your shoulder against this thing while I tighten it up?"

Milton couldn't help but like this man. He was over thirty years older than Milton and lot smarter and wiser, but he never seemed to get stressed out. Scott was a big man with a grey, grizzly beard and not much hair. He also had an easy, calm way about him that caused almost everybody in the shop to like him.

Milton hated the job, but he loved working with Scott. Scott was like the father Milton had never had.

"What do you and Carol have going on this weekend?" Scott asked as he tightened one of the nuts holding the lift mechanism onto one of the state's large trucks they were servicing in the cavernous garage.

Milton was reluctant to answer. Finally he said, "She does her thing, and I do mine."

"Have you tried to find things you can do together?" Scott suggested.

"Well…yeah," Milton returned. "I used to invite her to go with me to the bar to watch the Auburn games with the guys, but she was never much of a football person."

"I'm sure there are other things that she might enjoy doing with you."

"I appreciate what you're trying to do, Scott, but to be honest, things aren't going well with me and Carol right now."

"I'm sorry to hear that," Scott returned sincerely.

"I wish we had a great marriage like you and Phyllis," Milton continued, "but we don't. She's been mad at me ever since I lost my job as a salesman with Dexter Flooring."

"Why is that?"

"Because it had the potential to be a pretty good job, but I blew it," Milton said, hanging his head. "Carol has her heart set on having a family. Personally, I don't want any kids. But now that I've lost the good job and I'm stuck in this one, we can't afford a family. Carol thinks that's why I dropped the salesman job. But the truth is, Scott, that I was a crummy salesman. Honestly, I've failed at about everything I've ever tried."

"You're a pretty good mechanic," Scott said encouragingly.

"Well, I grew up tinkering with car engines, but any success I've had here is because I work with you."

Just then an alarm bell rang.

"Finally it's five o'clock!" Milton exclaimed. "This week is over!" Milton started to walk toward the office to pick up his paycheck.

"Hey, Milt!" Scott called firmly. "Before you leave how about helping me put away the tools and straighten up a bit? The company likes it when we take care of their stuff."

"Oh…uh…right…I'm sorry. I'm just anxious to get out of here."

After their area was swept and the tools put away, the two men joined the other mechanics and helpers as they marched up to the office window to receive their paychecks.

"Say, Milton," Scott began, "Phyllis and I are having a cookout at the house tomorrow with some friends. We'd love for you and Carol to join us! It might be a good thing for y'all. Phyllis and I would love to meet your wife."

"Oh…uh…thanks, Scott. That would be great, except…uh…I'm meeting up with my ol' frat brothers to watch the game tomorrow. Maybe some other time."

After Milton pulled into the driveway of his small rental house, he walked through the side door and straight to the refrigerator.

"Is that you?" Carol called from the bedroom.

"What happened to all the beer?" Milton returned.

"I thought you were going to pick up some more on your way home," Carol shot back.

"I tried, but the card didn't work."

"Milton, no!" Carol gasped as she walked into the kitchen. "You didn't max out another card, did you?"

"I'm not the only one who buys stuff," Milton shot back defensively.

"Did you get paid today?" Carol asked.

"Yeah. What about it?"

"Give me your check, Milton."

"WHAT? I'm not giving you my check! You've got your own check. This is MY money!"

"Milton, we talked about this!" Carol returned anxiously. "We live off my money, and we pay bills with yours. We are too far behind in our payments!"

"THIS WHOLE THING STINKS!" Milton yelled, slamming the refrigerator door. "I AM SICK OF WORKING LIKE A DOG ALL WEEK AND NOT BEING ABLE TO DO ANYTHING THAT I WANT! I CAN'T LIVE LIKE THIS!"

"Don't yell at me!" Carol returned in anger. "I don't like this anymore than you do!"

"You don't understand what I'm going through!" he shot back in desperation, rubbing his hands through his hair.

All his feelings of failure came to a head at that moment and pushed Milton towards his favorite coping strategy…escape.

"I'm sorry, Milton, but it has to be this way."

"NO, IT DOESN'T!" he snapped and stormed out the door.

Milton needed cash, but the bank was always closed by the time he got off work, so he pulled into the parking lot of a tiny, bright yellow building with the name 'Quick Cash' over the door.

"I need you to cash my check," he said to the rough-looking guy behind the desk.

"Let's see," said the man, studying the check Milton had dropped on his desk. "You're take home is seven hundred thirty-seven dollars and sixty-four cents. I'll give you six hundred and twenty."

"WHAT?" Milton screamed. "YOU'RE TAKING OVER A HUNDRED OUT OF IT!"

"Fees, man, fees," the man returned, uncaring. "Take it or leave it."

Without waiting for an answer, he turned the check over and tossed a pen toward Milton. He tapped rudely on the back of the check, indicating that Milton was to endorse it.

"You're a crook!" Milton growled as he signed the check.

The cash was quickly counted and was just as quickly snatched up by Milton. Twenty minutes later he was still angry both at the man and at himself when he pulled into Bernie's Sports Bar.

It was well after midnight when he arrived back at his house. He was pretty sure Carol had gone to bed, so he flopped down onto the couch and pulled the afghan over him. If he tried to climb in bed, he'd most likely wake her up, and he didn't want to deal with another argument. Life wasn't good, but at least for a few hours he had escaped the stress.

Chapter One

Chapter Two

The next morning Milton was startled awake by the loud growl of the blender as Carol made her smoothie.

"Did you brew some coffee?" he asked as he shuffled into the kitchen.

"The stuff's in the cabinet if you want some," she answered coldly. She picked up her smoothie and suddenly turned to face her husband. "Listen, Milt, we have got to talk about our finances! You can't keep doing this!"

"I know, Honey. I know. I'm sorry, but I'll go crazy if I can't go blow off some steam! Just give me this weekend, and I'll do better."

"You have to, Milton! We can't make it like this!"

"Alright…alright…You got my word on it. Are you going out?"

"I'm meeting Becky and one of her friends to walk at the park. I guess you're meeting the guys."

"Yeah," he answered rummaging in the cabinet for the coffee. "We'll be at Bernie's till the game's over."

"Please, Milton, be careful what you spend. We're desperate!"

"OKAY, CAROL! DON'T NAG ME!"

As soon as Milton Collins stepped through the door at Bernie's, he heard his name. "Milty, ol' buddy! War Eagle!" This was said by a grinning man in a Hawaiian shirt and khaki shorts who was sitting at the bar and lifting a partially consumed glass of beer.

"Hey, Blake. War Eagle," Milton said with a wave as he walked over to join his friend, signaling to the bartender to bring him a beer as well.

"So, my friend, how is life in paradise? *Heh, heh!*" Blake Miller asked with a chuckle as he raised his beer in a mock toast.

"Not so good," Milton admitted. "Carol's mad that I'm not earning as much as I did."

"You should have listened to me," Blake returned pompously, taking a sip from his drink.

"I told you that sales job was a great opportunity. Man, sales is where it's at!"

"If I had your confidence, maybe I could have made it work," Milton responded. "But the truth is that I'm a terrible salesman. I'm actually relieved to not be doing it anymore, but it's made my home life miserable."

"Collins," a gruff voice called from the other side of the room. "Come over here!"

"Hold onto your wallet," Blake whispered with a grin as Milton rose to join the man at the table. "Sid's setting up the Iron Bowl trip to Auburn."

"Are you going?" Milton asked.

"Wouldn't miss it for the world!" Blake returned excitedly. "It's the best thing we do all year…especially if we win! You gotta go, Milty! Trips like this with your best buds is what life's all about! It doesn't get any better than that!"

With a nod Milton walked over to join his friend at the table covered with papers. "Hey, Sid, what's up?" Milton said cheerfully.

"What's up?" Sid shot back gruffly. "What do you think is up? I'm trying to get this Auburn trip put together for you guys because none of the rest of you lazy slobs will take the time to do it!"

"We appreciate what you do, Sid," Milton said apologetically. "You do a great job."

"Stick a sock in it!" Sid snapped back. "I've just had to deal with Pete and all of his whinin'. Now, are you goin' with us to the Iron Bowl this year or not? An' if you are, I need three hundred bucks from you today."

"Uh…yeah, I'm…I'm going," Milton said as he fished into his pocket for his roll of cash. Milton counted out the three hundred and then paused. He hesitated for a moment, then leaned closer to his friend and whispered, "Hey, Sid, remember that pill you let me try last time?"

"Yeah, how'd you like it?" Sid whispered back out of the side of his mouth.

"It was crazy," Milton said, glancing around, "but…uh…I need some more."

"A bag of five is a hundred bucks," Sid answered in a low voice without looking at his friend.

Milton laid another hundred onto the stack of money, and Sid slipped a small plastic bag under the table to his friend.

"Thanks," Milt whispered as he pocketed the pills and headed back to the bar.

"So do you like that new job of yours?" Blake asked offhandedly as Milton sat back down.

Milton sighed. "To be completely honest; no, I don't."

"Then why do it?" Blake shot back. "Find something you like an' do that. Life's too short to get stuck doing stuff you don't enjoy. 'The man who loves what he does never works a day in his life.' Look at me. I'm at the point in my life that if it's not fun, I'm not going to do it."

"Seriously?" Milton asked skeptically.

"Seriously!" Blake returned with confidence. "I've made that my life's motto. If it's not fun, then I won't do it!" Just then Blake's cell phone went off. When he saw who the call was from, he quickly added, "Except family.

"Hey, Nana! What's up?" Blake said as he answered the call. "Oh, just here with some friends watching the game…uh-huh…Are you kidding me? Is that today? Okay…Sorry, Nana. I'll be there as soon as the game's over. I promise…no, I really mean it this time. I'll be there when the game's over. Okay, bye…hmm? Oh, yeah…yeah, I love you too."

Blake looked at his friend and gave a heavy sigh.

When he saw the questioning look from Milton, Blake said, "Today's my grandmother's birthday. She made me promise a week ago that I'd show up. She's a persistent ol' bird. Nana's the only one in the family who genuinely cares about me, so I try to stay in touch with her. But she drives me crazy quoting the Bible to me and inviting me to all of her church stuff."

A little over three hours later, Blake pulled up to his grandmother's house. Edith Miller lived in a small white house with a well-cared for front yard that even had a white picket fence. Blake noticed a lot of cars parked out front and along the street.

Great! Blake said irritably to himself. *She probably has her whole Sunday school class in there.*

"Blakey!" a sweet voice called as he walked in the door.

"Hey, Nana!" Blake returned, surprised at the large crowd of people in the small house. "Happy birthday!"

"Thank you, dear," Edith returned, giving him a kiss on the cheek and taking him by the arm. "Come with me. I want you to meet all these friends of mine."

Resigning himself to his fate, Blake plastered a big, fake smile on his face and let himself be led around the room to meet each person. He was right—the Sunday school class was there, but also the group she played cards with, her walking friends, and her garden club friends. He met Mr. and Mrs. What-ever and Deacon Who-gives-a-rip until his eyes were starting to cross. Blake was just glad that he had thought to chew up half a box of breath mints before he came in in order to hide the alcohol smell.

Edith eventually sat Blake down with a husband and wife close to his age who were from her church. He actually was having an interesting conversation with them until he learned that the husband was an ardent Alabama fan, at which point Blake wanted to punch him in the face. Wisely, he excused himself while he was still smiling and went to the kitchen to get one of the Mountain Dews that his grandmother always kept in the fridge for him.

"So you're Blake?" a cheerful voice asked from behind.

Blake was still a little irritated from the last conversation and wanted to say, *Who wants to know?* But he pulled on his smile and nodded.

The man standing before him stuck out his hand and said, "I'm Jeff Simms. I'm the minister of your grandmother's church. Sister Edith has said so much about you."

Uh-oh, Blake thought to himself. *This could be bad. I wonder what this guy knows about me?*

In answer to his unspoken question Simms said, "She says you're quite a salesman."

A big grin spread across Blake's face. Finally, a subject he liked to talk about…himself.

"Heh, heh…Preacher, you don't know the half of it. Why, I could sell ketchup popsicles to a room full of ladies in white gloves!"

Blake was pleased to see that the laughter coming from Simms appeared to be genuine. They continued talking for a few more minutes, mostly consisting of Simms asking Blake about himself.

"I love your sense of humor and your quick comebacks," Simms returned, still laughing. "I understand now why your grandmother is so proud of you and loves you so much."

"Yeah, my Nana's awesome," Blake returned. "Best Nana in the whole world!"

"You know she worries about you too," Simms countered. "I know for a fact that she prays for you a lot."

"Well, she is my Nana. That's her job."

"I was wondering," Simms probed, "are her prayers working?"

"What are you talking about?" Blake snapped back, suddenly serious.

"I was wondering if you ever think about the condition of your soul."

"…MY SOUL?! WHO GAVE YOU THE RIGHT…"

Edith was in the dining room serving cake when she and everybody else heard the loud shouting and cursing coming from the kitchen.

"BLAKEY!" she yelled firmly when she stepped into the room.

Instantly Blake realized that he was way out of line. The effects of the beer, Auburn's frustrating loss, and his own short temper had caused him to let Simms push him over the edge. He gave the preacher one last glare, then turned humbly to face his disappointed grandmother.

"Nana...I'm sorry!" Blake began, seeing all the faces turned towards him. "I'm really, really sorry! I should never have come. I just need to leave." As he said this, he started to walk towards the front door, but Edith grabbed his arm as he walked by her.

"I think you're right," Edith said with tears forming in her eyes, "but I'll walk you out, Sweetheart.

"Faye," Edith called as they walked through the living room, "wrap up a large piece of that cake and bring it out to us, please."

"Nana, you don't have to do..."

"Hush, Blakey," Edith cut him off, squeezing his arm affectionately. "It's a chocolate cake, which I know is your favorite."

When they got to the end of her sidewalk, Blake turned to face his grandmother. "Nana, I'm so sorry I embarrassed you and messed up your party. It's just that the whole church and Bible thing isn't my life, and it drives me crazy when people try to push it on me."

"So I guess that means that I drive you crazy," Edith said with a smile.

"Sometimes," Blake smiled back, "but you're my Nana."

"I forgive you, Blakey," Edith said as Faye came hurrying up with the cake. Edith handed the treat to her grandson, looked him in the eyes, and said, "And I love you!"

"I don't know why," Blake smiled and kissed her on the forehead.

"I'm your grandmother," she answered firmly, "and because I'm your grandmother, that means that you and I are going to talk about your behavior tomorrow."

Chapter Three

Milton could hear the pounding on the door, but he couldn't make his body get up. His head was throbbing, and he felt like he was made out of lead—very nauseous lead. "Go away!" he yelled, but the pounding continued.

It was nearly five minutes later before he stumbled to the front door and unlocked it.

"Milton, you haven't been at work for three days!"

"Scott," Milton slurred as he staggered back towards the couch, "what're you doin' 'ere?

"You look terrible!" Scott said with concern. "Are you alright?"

"She left me, Scott!" Milton blurted out. "Can you believe it? She said she'd had enough, an' she jus' left."

"Did you come home drunk?" Scott asked sternly.

"Not drunk," Milton corrected with a smug grin, "at least, not mostly drunk. I was stoned. There is an exquisite difference between the two."

"No wonder she left you," Scott shot back. "She should have. You really messed up, Milton. You've lost your wife *and* your job. When you didn't come in or call two days in a row, the garage fired you."

"FIRED ME?!" Milton gasped.

"Well, what did you expect?"

"I...I don't know!" Milton stammered in confusion. "I didn't think..."

"That's right!" Scott shot back, cutting him off. "You didn't think, and it has cost you your wife and your job."

The truth finally started to sink into Milton's drug-fogged brain, and he began to cry. "OH, SCOTT," he sobbed, "I'M A TERRIBLE PERSON! I'VE RUINED MY LIFE AND CAROL'S! WHAT AM I GONNA' DO?"

"You've made a big mistake, buddy," Scott said compassionately, "but I'm going to try to help you."

"Thank you, Scott...thank you!" Milton replied, still crying.

"You're welcome, but you are going to have to start making better choices, and you're going to start by getting rid of the drugs. Do you have any of them left?"

"The bag's on the table," Milton slurred back.

Scott found the small plastic bag on the kitchen table and pulled out the one remaining pill. He tossed it down the kitchen sink, turned on the water, and flipped on the garbage disposal.

Next he searched the fridge, pulling out two bottles of beer and pouring them down the drain as well.

"When was the last time you had something to eat?" Scott asked when he walked back into the living room.

"Don't remember," came the answer.

"Well, I'm going to get you some coffee and something to eat. While I'm gone, you're going to take a shower and try to get yourself cleaned up. Come on!"

Scott grabbed Milton's wrist, and the powerful man lifted Milton to his feet and led him back to the bathroom. "Now take your clothes off and get in the shower."

"In a little bit," Milton said and dropped down sleepily onto the toilet. "You go ahead and go."

Scott growled and turned the cold water on in the shower. Then he effortlessly lifted Milton up and stood him under the blast of cold water, clothes and all. Milton began screaming and flailing his arms, but Scott held him in place.

"Let me out, Scott! Let me out!"

"Not until you start to sober up!"

"Okay…okay!" Milton finally agreed, sounding much more normal. "I'll take a shower." He began pulling off his wet clothes.

"Good," Scott returned. "While you're doing that, I will go get you something to eat. And then, you and I are going to have a long, hard talk."

The 'talk' actually lasted nearly four hours. Most of it was Milton explaining what had happened between him and Carol. He was so crushed and broken that he even surprised himself with his honesty.

As he finished, Milton concluded by saying, "I'm so selfish and stupid, Scott, and I've lost everything in my life that matters! The really sad part is that I know that given half a chance, I'd mess it all up again! What am I going to do?"

Scott Jones reached up and put a compassionate hand on his friend's shoulder. "Milton, you're right. Your life is an absolute mess right now, and you've got no one to blame but yourself. My friend, you've tried being the ruler of your own life, and it hasn't turned out very well."

"You can say that again!" Milton shot back sadly.

"So are you ready to let someone else direct your life now?" Scott asked.

"Well, they certainly couldn't do any worse than I have. Are you going to start helping me make decisions? Are you going to be my life coach?"

"You need somebody much better than me for that job," Scott answered with a laugh, "and you need more than a coach. You need a King over your life—a King Who loves you more than you love yourself—a King Who wants the best for you and Who never makes mistakes. Milton, you need Jesus."

"Is that what you and Phyllis did…make Jesus your King?"

"Yep," Scott nodded, "and it was the best decision we ever made."

"Jesus, huh?" Milton returned thoughtfully. "I'm ashamed to say it, but I really don't know much about Him."

"Then that's where we start," Scott said with confidence. "After I get off work tomorrow evening, I will come by and pick you up."

"Pick me up?" Milton asked with a questioning look. "Where are you taking me?"

"You are coming to my house for a good dinner, and then you and I are going to begin reading and discussing our way through the book of John in the Bible so you can learn about the King that you so desperately need."

From then on, twice a week Milton showed up at Scott's house to study the Bible. Scott invited several other men to join them in their discussions, and they became a support group for Milton.

When they finished the book of John, Milton asked Scott, "So if someone believed in Jesus, what would they do to be His follower?"

"I would tell them to follow Him," Scott said with a smile.

"No, I mean for real, Scott," Milton shot back. "After reading all this stuff about Jesus and seeing how He has changed you, Phyllis, and the guys in the group, I want that for me. No, I NEED Him in my life! I've decided that I don't want to go back to living my old life! I want to follow Jesus now, so what do I do?"

"Well, we've looked at the Bible to learn about Jesus," Scott answered, "so let's look at the Bible and see how the first disciples followed Him."

"So where do we go?" Milt asked eagerly as he picked up the Bible Scott and Phyllis had given him and opened it.

"The book of Acts," Scott answered with a smile. "It's time for us to study the book of Acts. Let's look at how God led those people to follow Jesus, and that will answer your question."

An hour later Milton sat back from his Bible and said, "So here in Acts chapter two, three thousand people wanted to be saved, and when they asked what to do, Peter told them to 'repent and be baptized'."

"So?" Scott asked

"Well, I'm a little confused," Milton answered. "I remember reading where Jesus said that people just need to believe, or something like that."

"That's true," Scott returned. "Hebrews eleven verse six says, *Without faith it's impossible to please God and whoever would draw near to God must believe that He exists and that He is a rewarder of those who diligently seek Him.*

"But these people in Acts two weren't told to believe," Milt argued.

"That's because they already believed in Jesus as the Messiah," Scott explained. "That's why it says that they were cut to the heart in verse thirty-seven. Peter didn't tell them to believe because they already had faith. He could tell that they were past that. They just needed to know how real faith was supposed to respond."

"By repenting of their sins and being baptized?"

"Exactly, Milt!" Scott returned. "Repenting of your sins and being baptized aren't works that earn you anything. They are simply faith responses to what you believe about King Jesus. James says in His book in the Bible that *faith without works is dead.* In other words, a faith that doesn't respond is not real faith. Peter expected the three thousand people he was preaching to who wanted to follow Jesus to spend the rest of their lives responding in faith to their new King; repenting and being baptized was where they were supposed to start."

A few days later Milton had Scott stop by his house after work. "You got to see this, Scott," Milton said excitedly as he led his friend into the kitchen. "I'm so proud of myself! Look at how great I'm doing!"

Milton pointed to a large piece of paper taped to the front of the refrigerator. Across the top of the paper was listed: Daily Bible Reading, Pray three times a day, Encourage Someone, Share Jesus, Bible Study, and Church. On the left side of the paper were listed the days of the month. In the center of the page were lots of check marks under the titles.

"See all I've been doing?" Milton asked enthusiastically. "What do you think?"

His friend studied the page for several moments. Finally he asked, "Milt, why are you doing this?"

"It's encouraging to me! It shows that I'm becoming a man of God!"

"Milt, doing these things doesn't make you a man of God. All they do is make you religious. A man of God does these things and more, but not to keep a list...not to prove that they're a good person. That's what the Pharisees did to show that they were better than everyone else. A real man or woman of God is all about loving God and His Son, Jesus Christ. Reading and studying the Bible, praying, encouraging others, sharing Christ, giving, worshiping God—those are all things that they do as an expression of their love for God and His Son. Jesus said, *He who has my commands and obeys them, he is the one who loves Me.*

"What does that mean?"

"It means, Milt, that our obedience is Jesus's love language. If you want to say *I love You* to God and Jesus, then do all those things and more, but not to keep a list. Do them as an expression of your love for God and His Son. When you encourage or bless others, Jesus said that He takes that as you doing it to Him. He said when you give to others in His name, you are actually giving to Him. That's how we express our love to Christ."

"But I'm used to thinking about myself all the time," Milton admitted. "So how do I learn to love Jesus more? How do I make it about Him and not me?"

"God's word says *we love because He first loved us.* Spend a lot of time looking at the cross. Jesus's sacrificial death on the cross for us is the greatest expression of love there is. When you see how much Jesus loves you, love for Him is the natural outgrowth of that."

Two weeks later during a meal with the Joneses, Phyllis turned to Milton. "I think you know how proud Scott and I are of your faith in Jesus and of the strong Christian man you are becoming, but have you told Carol about the new Milton?"

Milt hung his head at the question. "I tried, Phyllis. Honest, I have. But she won't pick up the phone. I guess she's still really upset with me, and I can't blame her. I treated her terribly and she didn't deserve that!"

"You have to keep trying," Scott encouraged. "She needs to know how hard you're working to change your life."

"Oh, I'll keep trying to get a hold of her," Milton returned earnestly. "Even if she can't forgive me, I've got to do everything in my power to try to make it right with her. Jesus wants me to do that. But, Scott, I'm not the one changing my life. Jesus is doing all of that, just like He said He would. I can't explain it, but it's the most amazing thing I've ever experienced!"

"Just don't quit, Milton," Phyllis urged. "It's really important that Carol knows what Jesus is doing in your life."

"Like I said, I tried earlier today," Milton returned. "Tomorrow I'm leaving for my trip to Auburn for the big game with Alabama with some of my fraternity brothers. I promise, Phyllis, I'll call her again as soon as I get back."

"Are you sure you should go?" Scott asked.

"I thought about not going," Milton answered. "I know it's not good for me to spend a lot of time with those guys. But they are my friends, and I don't want to just throw them out of my life. Besides, I've already paid for the trip."

"Just remember how far you've come," Scott urged. "Be strong! You don't want to do anything to hurt your relationship with Jesus."

"Don't worry, Milton answered with a smile. "I'm His, and He's mine."

Chapter Three

Chapter Four

"Hey, Harvey, what kind of plane is this?"

"My name is Harold, and it's a Beechcraft Bonanza."

"It looks kind of old."

"She was built in '95," Harold returned defensively, "but she's in great shape. Bonanzas last forever."

"Hmmm…You sure?"

"Listen," Harold snapped, on the verge of losing his cool over all the annoying questions, "I'm trying to finish my preflight here to make sure everything is safe and ready for this flight! If you want me to take you to Auburn, Alabama, this plane will get you there. If you have any questions about my aircraft or my ability to fly it, then let's call this off right now!"

"Sorry…sorry," the questioner apologized and quickly moved over to join his companions.

"Whew!" he said in a low voice. "Whatever you do, don't mess with Harley over there. That guy's a grouch! I was just trying to engage him in some friendly conversation, an' he about bit my head off!"

"Just leave him alone, Pete. He's trying to get the plane ready."

"Well, we're paying him for this trip," Pete shot back. "We're like his bosses, right? I mean, the least he can do is be polite to one of his bosses."

"Actually, Pete, you haven't paid me for your part of the trip yet. So that makes *us* his bosses...not you. So don't mess with my pilot."

"I told you, Sid," Pete whined uncomfortably, "I hurt my back, and I didn't get as many hours in this month. I'll pay you next month."

"Okay, so next month," Sid shot back, "you can come out here and yell at the pilot all you want."

"I wasn't yelling at him."

"Whatever," Sid cut him off. "Just leave the pilot alone! Where's Miller? Everybody was supposed to be here at the airfield by ten o'clock sharp!" This was said to Pete and two others who were standing together a short distance from the airplane. The only answer Sid got was two blank stares and a shrug.

"Friend of mine or not," Sid declared, "there's no way I'm letting him make us late getting to our seats at the Iron Bowl. We haven't missed a kickoff in eight years, and it's not gonna happen today!"

"He'll be here, Sid," Milton Collins said. "You know Blake. He's always late."

"Well, he has until the plane's ready," Sid shot back, "then we're leaving…with or without him!"

"Wait!" Milt called out. "Here he comes now!"

"Alright, all aboard!" the pilot called to the group.

"You cut it pretty close, Miller," Sid snarled as the newest member of the group trotted up.

"O come on, Sidneypoo," Blake said with an annoying smile. "You wouldn't know what to do with yourself if you didn't have someone to grouse at."

Sid pushed Blake away as his irritating friend pretended to kiss him on the cheek. "An' don't call me Sidney! You know I hate that! Now all of you get on the plane!"

The five friends quickly climbed into the Bonanza and found their seats. The pilot started the three hundred horsepower, turbo-charged engine and used the radio to check in with the airfield's flight control. After rechecking oil, gas, and rpm gages, he then set the desired frequency for his navigation radio and taxied out onto the runway.

"I wasn't sure you were actually going with us this year, Milt," Blake Miller said as he pulled a bottle of beer from the backpack at his feet. "You've missed a lot of our guys' nights over the last few months. We were starting to think you didn't love your ol' frat brothers anymore."

"I guess it has been a while since I've been with you guys," Milton said, not making eye contact. "I've really been through a whole bunch of junk since I saw you. A lot of things have changed for me recently."

"The last time you and I talked," Miller continued after taking a long pull from his drink, "you and your wife were having problems, an' you weren't doing too well at your mechanic's job."

"Yeah," Milt answered thoughtfully, "that was a really dark time. It actually got worse, you know. Toward the end, just before Carol left me, I started drinking hard and doing drugs. I lost my wife and my job. I guess my life was pretty black."

"You seem like you're doin' okay now," Miller returned.

"I'm doing a lot better. I met some people who pulled me out of a dark place and helped me see things differently."

"Like who?" Blake asked, his curiosity piqued.

Milton squirmed in his seat as the plane left the ground. He seemed uncomfortable answering the question. "Well, the first person was a fellow I worked with at the shop," Milton began. "He's an older guy, but he knows a lot about fixing things. He and I spent several days putting lifting devices on some of the trucks. He was always asking me stuff about myself, like he really cared about me."

"Be careful around fellows like that," Blake said cynically. "They'll take your money. I know about those kind of guys, Milt."

"Not this guy," Milton defended, "Scott's the real deal. When I got canned at work, Scott came by to check on me. He made sure I had food and just took the time to listen to me. He said that if I wanted to get my life straightened out, he would help me. I guess I was bad enough to ask for help. So Scott introduced me to several of his friends who have helped me a lot."

Blake reached into his backpack and pulled out a second beer, handing it to his companion.

Milton quickly drew back when he saw the offered drink. "Oh, uh, no thanks, man," he stammered. "I, uh, don't do that anymore...Too much chance I'll fall back into bad habits."

Blake just stared at his buddy suspiciously. Finally he replaced the beer and said, "Milt, what have you gotten yourself into? Are these a bunch of religious loonies? Are you in some kind of a cult?"

"No, it's not a cult or anything like that," Milton said defensively.

"But they are religious, right?" Blake shot back accusingly.

"Well...yeah, they're Christians."

"Milty, Milty, Milty!" Blake returned. "These people will ruin your life! I know! I've been around them! My grandmother's one of them! They're against most of the really fun stuff! Oh, I guess the whole church thing is okay for people like my grandmother, because that's about all she's got. But religion is a nuisance. It just gets in my way. Besides, I'm not convinced any of it is true."

"You got it all wrong, Blake," Milton answered. "My life is so much better now that I've started following Jesus! It's really amazing!"

"Hush, will you!" Blake urged, looking up at Sid in the front passenger's seat. "You know how Sid feels about religion. If he heard you just now, he'd cuss you out and never include you in any of our stuff again.

"Look, Milt, if you feel the need to join up with those people, that's your business. But if you want to hang around with your best buddies, you'd better keep all that to yourself. In this group it's better to follow the 'don't ask, don't tell' policy, if you know what I mean."

Milton gave his friend a confused look.

Blake rolled his eyes and explained, "We aren't going to ask, and you don't need to tell."

"I understand, Blake," Milton returned. "But I really mean it. All this has been wonderful for me. I have a great life now with people who genuinely care for me and help me stay on track. Scott even helped me get my job back, and I'm still hoping to get back together with Carol."

The two-and-a-half-hour flight went smoothly, and they were starting to descend toward a small airfield outside of Auburn where an Uber driver with a van was supposed to be waiting for them. Harold, their pilot, was just lowering the flaps on the wings to slow them down when suddenly he yelled. He threw up his arms involuntarily as a large flight of ducks smashed directly into the front of the plane. The windshield shattered, and the right engine thumped loudly and burst into flames. The Bonanza immediately nosed down and within seconds slammed into a forest of pine trees. Both wings ripped off, and the engines exploded while the fuselage plowed through the ground and the trees for another seventy feet before crashing into a large pine and tearing in half.

Chapter Five

Blake Miller opened his eyes and looked around. He remembered that he had been in a plane crash and that there had been an explosion as the plane hit the trees. He thought he recalled his seat tearing free when the body of the plane slammed to a stop, followed by a feeling of intense pain, and then…blackness.

So where am I? he thought. *I'm not hurting now. In fact, I seem to be perfectly fine.*

As he rose to his feet, Miller was surprised at how dark it was. He could barely make out the rocks and boulders nearby. Looking around, he spotted the crash scene not far away. It was burning fiercely, but none of the light from the fires illuminated anything around him. It was like he could see the light, but it couldn't get to him. He hurried over to find out if he could help any of his friends.

Suddenly Miller heard a chorus of shrieking laughter coming from the dark sky above, and it terrified him. Without thinking, he dropped behind a large boulder to his left. As he peeked around the rock, Blake was stunned to see three large, winged figures land beside the burning wreckage. "I'm either drunk or dreaming!" Miller gasped as he watched.

The three figures were human-like in their appearance. They had hands and feet, but their fingers and toes were longer than a human's and ended with long, fierce-looking claws. Their faces seemed to be permanently contorted into an expression of terrible, sneering hatred, and their eyes glowed yellow.

As Blake watched, the three hideous figures prepared to wade into the wreckage, but before they could, an intense beam of light illuminated the three. This light seemed to terrify them, and they leaped to the side, covering themselves with their wings. As they did so, two other winged figures, equally as large, landed in the center of the light where the first three had stood.

These two looked totally different from the first ones. Blake could see that one of them was powerfully built and had skin the color of bronze. The other was shorter and thinner with silver-colored skin. Though smaller than the first, this second figure was also a powerful-looking personage.

Ignoring the three who cowered nearby, the two stepped into the wreckage and, with smiles on their faces, lifted Milton out of the carnage. Milton smiled too and seemed uninjured. The two powerful beings each took one of Milt's arms and, still surrounded by the radiant beam of light, sprang into the air and flew away with Blake's friend. From behind the boulder, Miller watched as the beings of light carried Milton in the direction of a bright, glowing radiance far away. As Blake stared hard at the distant sight, he was able to tell that it was actually a huge, illuminated city that appeared to be floating just above the horizon.

After Milton and his rescuers had left and the intense beam of light had disappeared, the first three beings leapt to their feet and, with a nervous laugh, charged into the wreckage of the crash. Suddenly Blake heard yelling and screaming, and a pair of the beings came back out gripping the pilot and two of Blake's friends. All of the victims were shouting and bawling in terror. Just then the third repulsive creature stepped out of the fire dragging Sid, who fought, screamed, and cursed, but all to no avail. The terrifying creature who gripped him only laughed ghoulishly. With a shout from this last being, the three spread their large wings and launched into the air, flying off with their four captives. The awful screaming coming from the pilot and Blake's friends was terrifying. The group did not fly toward the city of light. They flew off into the darkness and disappeared over a distant hill.

When Blake found himself alone, he was stunned by what he had seen. Climbing from behind his boulder, Blake shuffled over to the crash. Looking into the shattered remains of the plane, Blake was horrified to see the bodies of his four friends and the pilot.

Just then Blake heard faint shrieks of terror from multiple voices coming out of the darkness some distance away. The sound of it made his knees weak, and he stumbled back to the boulder.

"WHAT IS GOING ON?" he shouted to himself. "I MUST be dreaming! I MUST be!" In response Blake began slapping his face hard in an effort to wake himself up.

"Do you know how foolish you look doing that?"

The deep voice so close by shocked Blake, and he spun around to identify the source. Before him were the same two beings of light he had seen carry off Milton.

"Please don't hurt me!" Blake begged as he backed against the boulder.

"We aren't here to hurt you," the silver-skinned person answered. "Our Master sent us to try and protect you from the demons for as long as we can."

"DEMONS? That's ridiculous!" Blake shouted, dumbfounded. "I...I don't believe in demons."

A smile broke out on the faces of both giant beings at hearing Blake's confession. "You saw them carry off the others," the silver-skinned one answered. "What do you think they were?"

"I don't know!" Blake said, rubbing his face. "I don't know what I saw! This...this could just be a bad dream!"

"Well, as soon as they finish tormenting the others and eventually cast them into the pit of fire, your 'bad dream' is coming back for you."

"Why? Why are they coming for me? I haven't done anything to them!"

"They own you," the silver one returned. "You belong to them."

The larger bronze giant nodded in solemn agreement.

"They may come back and look for me at the crash," Blake shot back, "but they won't find me. Somehow I got out."

"Actually, you didn't," the silver one, who was obviously the main spokesman, said.

"Of course I did! I'm standing right here!"

"The seat you were strapped into," the silver one said, "was torn from the flying machine, and you are still in it. There you are lying in that brush over there."

Following the pointing arm of the giant, Blake was stunned to see his body, still in his seat, lying in the thick brush not far from the burning plane. Blake Miller stared at his severely injured self, trying to make sense of what was happening. Finally he asked in fear, "Am I...dead?"

"No," the shining one answered. "See, you've still got your silver cord."

Confused, Blake followed the speaker's pointing hand and saw a thin line of shimmery light coming from his side and winding along the ground to the injured figure lying in the brush.

"What is this?" Miller asked in confusion and began to yank at the shiny string of light.

"Now we *know* you're foolish," the winged stranger said with a chuckle. His large quiet companion also gave a snicker through his nose.

"That's your life line, human! When that comes off, you WILL be dead."

"So what are you telling me?" Blake demanded angrily. "You say I'm not dead, but when I take a peek over there, I see myself bleeding out in those weeds. I look pretty dead to me! Why am I even standing here looking at myself with this crazy extension cord stuck in me? And what happened to my friends? I need some answers from you two, and I need them now!"

"Answers must wait," the bronze giant rumbled as he looked into the dark distance. "The demons are returning."

"Barcos, cover the life line!" the silver one called urgently and quickly spread his large wings over Blake and himself. Barcos, the larger one, gave a powerful sweep of his wings, blowing up a cloud of black, cinder-like dust that effectively covered the shimmery cord coming from Blake. Then he too shielded himself with his great wings. As soon as his wings came together, they took on the appearance of the boulders around them.

An instant later three demons landed by the wreckage. They searched through the broken metal, ignoring the flames. "There's no one else here!" one of them snapped. "This is the second time we've done this and found nothing!"

"Where is he, Rage?" a second one demanded. "You said the boss ordered us to pick up five for the pit!"

"How should I know?" Rage snarled back. "We got all there was except for that believer the angels grabbed. Maybe the boss got the number wrong."

"Well, if there's another one here an' we missed 'im," the second demon shot back, "I'm tellin' the boss it was because of you!"

"Yeah, you would too," Rage growled angrily. "Alright then, spread out and start looking!"

Chapter Six

Milton Collins knew he was dead, and yet he had never felt more alive. The two angels who had carried him here from the plane crash told him that their Master, King Jesus, had sent them.

He remembered that it had been dark around the crash site, but he and the angels had been illuminated in a beam of light that came from above. The two had lifted him off the ground effortlessly and rapidly flew with him toward the source of the light, which Milton had seen was a gorgeous city that sparkled and shone like a chest of beautiful gems. The closer they got the more amazing it looked.

"Wh...what's all that noise?" he had asked as they drew closer to the city.

"That, Milton, is your welcome home party," the silver one had said with a smile. "They are all here for you."

"But I don't know anybody here," Milton had returned, "except maybe Jesus."

"Well, they know you!"

The two angels landed softly, placing Milton on a wide, paved road that was golden-tinted and as clear as glass. He was standing in front of a massive gate that was round, shimmery white, and ornately carved. Lining each side of the lane leading to the open gate was an enormous crowd—each person looking at him and cheering, jumping, and laughing with all their strength.

As Milton began walking up the lane, he burst out laughing just from the pure joy of the crowd. He had no idea who these people were, but they were all calling his name, waving to him, and shouting welcomes. The enthusiasm of the people never waned as he walked toward the gate. If anything it, got even more jubilant. When he stood in the opening of the massive entry, he turned back to look at the throng. They had closed in behind him but were still cheering just as hard.

Then suddenly they all stopped. Milton sensed that someone was behind him, and he turned around. He saw a man standing nearby with the most loving, radiant smile he had ever seen. When Milton looked into His eyes, the only way he could describe them was supremely happy. He had white hair, wore a white robe that seemed iridescent as it shone, and across his chest was a wide golden sash.

"You're Him!" Milton gasped.

In response Jesus simply nodded, and His smile got bigger.

"I have waited a long time for you, Milton," Jesus said genuinely. "I called to you for many years, but you were too preoccupied and too focused on yourself to listen."

Milt hung his head at the truth of these words.

"When you started hurting, you turned to alcohol and drugs instead of to me. I was still calling when you lost your job and Carol, but again you weren't listening. That's when I sent my servant Scott to help you and point you to Me because I'm the One who truly loves you and the only One Who could help. And that's when you listened. You finally heard My voice, chose to come to Me, and believe in Me, and I'm so glad you did!

"I gave My life for you, and you finally gave your life to Me. So now I am excited to say to you, well done, Milton Hamilton Collins, My good and faithful servant. I welcome you into the joy of your Lord!"

As Jesus made this announcement, the massive crowd again erupted into roaring cheers.

"But, Lord," Milton began with tears in his eyes, "I've sinned so much, and been so weak, and was so foolish and ignorant…"

"None of that matters now, dear friend. It has all been fully paid for." As Jesus said these words, He extended his hands to Milton to show him the nail prints in His wrists.

"Put shoes on his feet and bring the robe that has been made especially for him!" Jesus called.

Three angels suddenly appeared above them, one holding a pair of golden shoes and two holding a beautifully embroidered white robe. With a nod from Jesus, the angels dropped down. One released the shoes, and they suddenly appeared on Milton's feet.

Wow!" Milton exclaimed. "I can't believe it! These things feel so good! It's like they're a part of my feet."

"You'll love them!" Jesus answered with a smile.

The other two angels brought the robe and helped Milton put it on.

"Oh, Lord, it's so beautiful!" Milton said as he admired it.

"It was designed and made just for you," Jesus returned with a grin. "There's not another like it."

As Milton excitedly examined his special robe, Jesus called out again, "Put his ring on his hand!"

Again an angel appeared holding a black onyx case with golden edges. The angel opened the lid to the case, and a gorgeous golden ring rose up and floated straight onto Milton's finger. It seemed to be made of gold, but it was brighter than any gold Milton had ever seen. The band and the setting were carved with delicate designs, and set in the center of the ring was a large, flat, white stone that shimmered hypnotically when Milton looked at it. He was stunned at the beauty of the gift. Lifting his hand, Milton stared into the depths of the stone's shimmery radiance. As he did so, a name suddenly appeared across the shiny surface. "It says 'Son of Compassion.'"

"No one can read your stone but you," Jesus explained. "That is the special name that I have given you."

"But why *Son of Compassion?*"

"Because you have received very little mercy or compassion in your life in the land of shadows," Jesus answered. "You know very well what that's like, and that's why you appreciated so much the mercy and compassion that I have shown to you. Everyone who comes here brings many sorrows and hurts, just as you have brought yours, but this is a place of healing and great comfort. There are many here who will delight in helping you heal and be comforted. Later, when the opportunity arises, you, Son of Compassion, will give great mercy and sympathy to those still to come."

"Bring his crown!" Jesus called out again, and another angel appeared, holding a beautifully designed band of gold that was placed on an embarrassed Milton's head.

"*Heh, heh!* You'll get used to it," Jesus chuckled as He put His arm around the newest citizen of Paradise.

"Lord," Milton asked with concern as he looked at his hands, "what is this bluish smoke swirling out of my fingers?"

"My Holy Spirit in you is visible here," came the answer.

"This is the Holy Spirit?"

"He is not limited by time or place," Jesus answered. "You will see My Spirit everywhere, and you will see that He loves you as much as the Father and I love you.

"Now walk with Me, My dear friend. Our Father wants you to come before Him."

As he and Jesus traveled further into the beautiful city of light, Milton was amazed at everything. Even the air had a fresh purity to it. Stunning fragrances wafted everywhere, and every breath he took seemed to give him strength and a feeling of power.

The streets were not just straight. They curved, and sometimes they widened out into large circles. The buildings were grand and glorious, some with magnificently and ornately carved columns. Everywhere were beautiful trees, shrubs, and flowers.

Milton was amazed at how quickly they traveled. They were walking, but it was like they were flying along the streets. There was a mountain in the center of the city, and they rapidly journeyed up the golden streets that led to the top. Once there Milton saw a gorgeous pavilion made completely of light. The love and joy radiating from it was intense and almost more than Milton could endure.

"Hold My hand," Jesus said with a smile as He led Milton into the presence of His heavenly Father.

Chapter Six

Chapter Seven

Blake Miller remained crouched under the spread wings of his rescuers for quite some time.

"Hey, shiny dude," Miller complained, "how about letting me out of your winged igloo. I need to stretch my legs."

"Keep your voice down, foolish one," the large being returned in a low voice. "The demons are not nearby right now, but they are still searching the area for you."

"Well, I'm starting to get cramps. So how about opening up your wings and let me stand up for a while?"

"Just wait."

"Why?"

"Unless you wish to be tortured mercilessly," the silver one answered, "you need to stay where you are for now. You humans can be so impatient!"

"You said that I'm not dead," Blake questioned, "so where am I? What is this place? And who are you and the big guy?"

"Some people in the shadow world where you come from refer to this place as Gehenna," the silver one began. "We have a different name for it, but it is a place of waiting for those who have died but who have not trusted in my Master."

"So I AM dead," Miller reasoned.

"All of your companions in the flying machine are, but you are still alive, though it is clear that without help you will not be alive long. It is because you are still alive that, at least for the moment, you are stuck here. As long as you have your life line, the demons can torture and torment you, but they cannot throw you into the pit of fire."

"Pit of fire?" Blake asked suspiciously.

"Just beyond that low hill in the distance is the beginning of it. It is a very large and expansive pit that's filled with flames, and there is no way out of it. All of those from your world who die without my Master are cast into the pit as they wait."

"Wait for what?" Blake asked again.

The silver one just stared at the man. "For the final judgment, of course."

"Final judgment," Miller scoffed. "Alright, listen up, shiny dude. I've finally figured this whole, weird thing out. As far as I'm concerned, all of this, including you, is just a bad dream. I'm going to wake up in a few minutes when we land in Auburn and head to the most important football game all year. And there's nothing you or the big guy can say to change my view on that.

"You being here doesn't make any sense. That means it can't be true, no matter how real it seems. If something doesn't make logical sense, I'm not going to believe it. So I'm telling you right now that I don't believe in you or those demon whatevers or the fiery pit OR your master. And that's another thing that makes no sense: why are you even here 'protecting me' since I'm not one of your 'believers'?"

"My Master sent us to do what we could to protect you for as long as we can because of the prayers of your grandmother for you."

"My GRANDMOTHER?" Blake gasped. "How do you know her?"

"In the place of shadows, Lady Edith is a great warrior for my Master."

"Lady Edith? Are you talking about Edith Miller? The Edith Miller who lives at 132 Bates Circle?"

"My Master has great respect for her," the silver one returned. "She asks daily for my Master to help you. That's what we were sent to do, at least until your body dies. At that point your future will be sealed, and Barcos and I will no longer be able to do anything to assist you."

"So you're just waiting for me to die, is that it?" Miller shot back.

"Actually we are trying to keep you out of the claws of the enemies long enough for someone in the land of shadows to find your injured body and save your life."

Suddenly the being folded his wings and stood up, saying, "The demons are further away now, so it would be safe for you to stand for a while."

Giving a groan, Blake also pushed upright and stretched his back and arms.

"You said that the big guy's name is Barcos," Miller observed, "but who are you?"

"I am Tirian," the silver one said with a slight bow of his head. "Barcos and I are warriors in the King's Host and Guardians of the Faithful."

"Guardians?" Blake asked with a suspicious look on his face.

"People in your world would call us angels," Tirian responded.

"Angels...right," Blake Miller snorted and laughed sarcastically. "Wow! I have never had a dream this vivid.

"So you two are my guardian angels?" Blake chuckled.

"No," Tirian returned. "We were Milton Collins's guardians, but when he died in the crash of the flying machine, we then took him to the city of Paradise to be with his Master and the other followers of our Master as they wait."

"Wait?"

"For the final..."

"Oh, right, right, right...the final judgment."

"Once Barcos and I delivered Milton Collins, our Master wanted to honor your grandmother's prayers. So we were sent to try to protect you as long as your body remains alive."

"Well," Miller said as he looked around at his surroundings, "isn't there some nicer place where we can wait for me to wake up rather than this dark wilderness? I don't know if you guys have noticed, but it stinks here. It smells like burning garbage. Listen, if this is going to take much longer, why don't you and ol' Barcos haul me off to Paradise over yonder? It's too far away to see it very well, but it sure looks nicer than this dump. Maybe I can get a beer there while I wait."

"You are not allowed in The City of Light," Tirian returned firmly. "Only those who love and follow my Master can enter Paradise. Those who don't must remain here."

"Okay, well, if those are the rules, then can't you guys do something to improve our situation here?"

Suddenly Barcos's arm shot up. "Demons coming back," he announced. "They're bringing more with them this time."

"How does he know that stuff?" Blake demanded. "Does he have some kind of 'spidey sense' or something?"

"We need to move further away," Tirian announced. "There are some low cliffs behind us. Let's take him there, Barcos."

The angels led him over and around a number of large and jagged boulders as they climbed up the steep slope. Finally Blake stopped and leaned against a rock wall, breathing hard.

"Listen, guys," he huffed. "You're both angels, and this is my dream, so why don't you two fly me up to the top of this steep hill before I have a heart attack?"

His companions stopped climbing and turned to look at him. Blake could see no sympathy in their eyes.

"People do have heart attacks in dreams, you know!"

"If we fly, the demons will see us and come and get you," Tirian returned. "Just keep climbing."

"Whew!" Miller huffed. "If I'm going to keep having dreams like this, I need to be in better shape."

"Here," Tirian announced when he drew near to the top of the hill. "I see a cave where we can hide you."

Blake was blowing hard when he reached the cave. The opening was just big enough to stand up in, and the cave itself was a single room about ten feet across and fifteen feet deep. Sitting down on a boulder in the back of the cave, Blake said, "You know, guys, it's pretty dark in this hole. Is there any way we can have some light in here?"

Tirian sighed and shook his head in annoyance. Finally he said to his companion, "Barcos, will you block the cave entrance while I provide some light for our charge?"

In response to his companion's request, the larger angel stood in the opening and spread his great wings, blocking all light from outside. Then Tirian held his hand in front of himself, and suddenly a ball of bright light appeared, floating above his hands, fully illuminating the entire cave.

"Well, that's a handy little trick," Miller smirked. "Can you get the History Channel on that thing?"

Tirian just glared at him.

"I didn't think so," Miller returned with a roll of his eyes.

"Barcos and I are not human," the silver angel began, "and because of that, we don't really understand how humans think, but it seems to me that you aren't taking this situation seriously."

"Why should I?" Miller answered casually.

"Because your life is quite literally being held by a thread," Tirian said as he nodded toward the thin, shiny cord that trailed from Blake's side, "and that thread is the only thing keeping you from the pit of fire."

"Oh, right…the pit of fire," Miller returned, making a pretend scary face. "Listen, silver dude…"

"Tirian."

"Whatever…The reason I'm not taking this seriously is because it's not! This doesn't happen in real life! YOU don't happen in real life! No offense, but you and the big guy are not the most pleasant dream characters to look at. This whole thing would be more fun if you two would turn into a couple of dancing girls."

"You are such a foolish and disrespectful human," Tirian said sternly.

"*Now* you're starting to sound like my grandmother," Miller snapped. "I'd try to be nicer — if it mattered, but in a dream, it doesn't. So suck it up!"

"Any moment your life could end," Tirian tried again, "and your attachment to the shadow world will terminate. At that point we can no longer protect you. The demons will snatch you up, do unspeakable horrors to you, and eventually cast you into the pit of fire. There you will remain until time ends and the final judgment occurs."

"Oh, yeah?" Blake sneered. "And then what happens? Oh, I know! Then God throws all the bad little boys like me into hell, right? Well, the problem with all of that is that there isn't any God, and there isn't any hell! I've seen through the scam! All that was cooked up originally by crooked, manipulative conmen who invented religion to use people's fears to control them. It has definitely worked over the years. Believe me, I know a great sales pitch when I see one. But no one's controlling me with all that snake oil! I'm too smart for that. I've seen the hypocrisy, and it's not going to work with me! Do you hear? Not with me!"

Chapter Eight

"Listen to me, human," Tirian began.

"My name's Blake," he shot back disrespectfully, interrupting the angel, "Blake Miller."

"Listen to me, Blake Miller," the angel continued. "If Barcos and I leave, the demons will find you. Though your life line will keep them from throwing you into the pit of fire for now, they will still torture you until your body in the shadow world dies, at which point they will throw you into the fiery pit. Then it gets worse!

"The only reason my friend and I are here is because our Master heard the prayers of your grandmother, who is a follower of our Master. He is showing compassion to her and to you. If you refuse to respect us because of our Master, the least you could do is respect the love your grandmother has for you."

On hearing this, Miller rolled his eyes and sighed. "You're right," Miller finally agreed. "My Nana does deserve my respect, if for no other reason than that, in her own deluded and weird way, she loves me. She always has, and I guess she always will."

"Lady Edith is a great woman," Tirian returned respectfully.

"Actually, with all of her religious mumbo jumbo, she's kind of a nut," Blake shot back, "though she is a sweet and loving nut. But she drives me crazy, always quoting the Bible to me and trying to get me to go to church with her. Do you know what those places are like?"

Both angels just stared at him.

"Oh, yeah…I guess you do.

"Well, religion is fine for her. After PaPa died, that's pretty much all she's got left. But I've got my whole life ahead of me."

Tirian pointed to Blake's silver cord and said, "Maybe not."

Jerking the cord away from the angel, Blake stood up. "Okay, listen. You and Barcos want to help me out, right? You've got me all tucked away and protected from the bad guys right here in this nice cave. So why don't you two fly back to your master and have him send an ambulance to the crash? Surely he's got a cell phone or something. That sounds like a great plan to me. So you guys go do that, and I'll just cool my heels right here in this safe ol' cave while you're gone. The medics will come, get me all taken care of, and I can wake up and get to the game. Then you guys can get on with doing your little angel thing. How about that? Does that sound like a plan or what?"

Tirian thought on this for a moment. Finally he said to his friend, "Barcos, it would be good to get help for his injured self as soon as possible. You fly back to the Master and request He send the medical help."

"Whoa, whoa, whoa," Blake interrupted. "Now ol' buddy Barcos here is a buff dude, and I'm sure he can hold his own one on one with the demons, but what if he runs into a bunch of them? He's gonna need help. You need to go with him. They'll never find me here. I'm perfectly safe in this great cave you found. So both of you go to be sure the message gets through."

Tirian looked less than convinced, so Blake played his trump card. "Nana would want you to."

Finally Tirian nodded his head in agreement. "Alright, but you must remain in this cave until we get back. Once the helpers from the land of shadows arrive, we will escort you down to them."

"You got yourself a deal!" Blake answered enthusiastically and stuck out his hand to shake on it. The two angels ignored his offered hand and immediately shot out of the mouth of the cave.

"Good night, Irene!" Blake exclaimed. "I never thought I would get rid of those two." Taking a quick look around outside the cave, he immediately began climbing down the hill and back to the wreckage.

So all I have to do, Blake thought to himself as he carefully descended the steep rocky hillside, *is to get close to the plane and be ready to go when the medical people arrive. When they get here and start taking care of me, I'm sure I'll finally wake up and be done with this crazy dream.*

Drawing close to the scene of the crash, Miller saw red lights flashing.

"Whoa! That was fast!" Blake said out loud as he watched the emergency people search the wreckage.

He observed them as they carefully extracted his friends' bodies from the twisted metal, but no one seemed to realize that he was lying injured in the brush a short distance from the others.

"HEY, YOU GUYS!" he shouted and waved his arms to get their attention. "YOU'RE MISSING ONE! HE'S RIGHT HERE IN THESE WEEDS! CAN'T YOU SEE?"

Apparently the medical people couldn't see. They couldn't hear either because no one noticed Blake's calls or movements.

"OH, COME ON, YOU GUYS! I'M LAYING RIGHT HERE!" Miller yelled, flapped his arms, and jumped up and down frantically.

One time as he landed, he accidently stomped on the silver cord, jerking the end attached to his injured self. Immediately the injured Blake groaned, and one of the emergency medical people stopped and turned to listen.

Seeing what had happened, Blake dropped to his knees and grabbed the cord, pulling it tight. He didn't want to pull it loose, so he tugged on it gently. As he did so, another groan came from the figure in the brush.

Blake could tell that the rescuer was moving curiously toward the sound but as yet had not spotted Blake's injured form. *Okay, he's walking in the right direction,* Miller thought excitedly. *I'll tug one more groan out of me, and then he'll find me.*

Just then Miller was startled with a chorus of piercing screams, and he was grabbed by his arms with a vice-like grip. A gang of ten demons landed around him, all laughing and shouting in victory at finally capturing their prey. Even though the noise the creatures made was deafening, the rescuers didn't seem to notice.

Miller was unable to move his arms, but he still gripped the silver cord and was able to jerk on it. Once more a groan escaped the lips of his injured self.

The demon holding Miller noticed the hand movement and quickly spotted Blake's semi-conscious body in the brush. "There he is — covered over in the brush!" the demon snarled loudly to the others. "That's why you air heads couldn't find him before. Now the sneaky bugger is pulling on his life line to try to attract help."

"It looks like it's workin' too, boss," another demon answered back. "One of them shadowlanders is headed straight towards where he's layin'."

"Here, hold 'im, Fang," the boss demon gripping Blake ordered and shoved his captive at another demon. "I'll take care of this!"

Miller immediately felt sharp, intense pain as the new captor's claws sunk into his arms from its powerful grasp. Blake gasped in shock, not just at the sharp pain but more so that he was feeling this kind of agony in what he thought was a dream.

The boss demon stepped between the rescuer and the brush where the injured Blake was hidden. The huge servant of Satan spread his wings and began flapping them furiously.

The medical worker was moving closer to where he thought he had heard a sound when suddenly he was hit by a fierce blast of wind that blew him backward and almost knocked him down.

"Let's get out of here!" One of the other rescuers yelled as the flames from the burning fuel began to be blown towards them.Quickly they gathered their equipment and hurried to the ambulances, departing with the bodies of the victims.

Though in intense pain, Blake watched in disappointment as the rescuers left the scene, having never seen his injured self. He knew police were probably nearby, but they would be keeping sight-seers away. No one would search the wreckage again until all the fires went out, and by then he knew that it would be too late.

As the rescuers left, the demons broke into a screaming victory dance. "TO THE PIT!" the boss yelled, and Blake felt himself jerked painfully off his feet as his evil captor launched into the black sky and carried him into the smelly darkness.

Chapter Nine

Milton was overwhelmed at the intensity of God's love for him…for HIM, of all people. But now he knew without a doubt that it was true, and he loved God and Jesus and the Holy Spirit more than he could ever say.

The joy that completely permeated the atmosphere in the presence of the Father was indescribable. God clearly delighted in being Himself. He absolutely delighted in His Son, Jesus. And for some strange reason that Milton couldn't comprehend, God delighted in him as well.

Milton had never been in such a joyful…fun place as when he was in the presence of the Father. Later Milton told himself that he should have known that being with God is so wonderful because, after all, everything that is good, all joy, and everything that is delightful was created by Him.

As Milton and his King walked down from the mountain, Jesus began to tell his friend about all the times in Milton's life when Jesus had reached out to him. He spoke of the things He loved the most about Milton and about the times when Jesus had cried with him. The young man leaned close as Jesus told him how He reached out to Milton through his difficult childhood.

Milton was amazed when Jesus recalled the tragedies of his life, then explained them from God's perspective. He was stunned to realize just how different his life looked when he saw it through God's eyes.

Once again Milton wasn't sure whether he and Jesus walked along the streets of gold or flew, but they traveled much faster than a car would have driven.

"It's the shoes," Jesus said with a sly smile. "Like I said, you're going to really love those shoes!"

They suddenly came to what appeared to Milton to be a massive city park. A rushing river flowed through the center of it, and there was luscious, manicured vegetation along both sides.

A man and a woman sitting on a beautifully carved, white bench beside the river rose to their feet as Jesus and Milton arrived.

Jesus turned to His companion and said, "You will enjoy getting to know everyone here, but I want you to meet these two first."

"Who are they, Your Majesty?"

"They are your grandparents and have been longing to meet you for some time. I'm going to leave you now and let the three of you get to know each other, but I will return soon." As He finished His words, Jesus was suddenly gone.

Turning to observe his approaching grandparents, Milton was stunned. By their appearance he judged that they couldn't be much older than he was.

"Milton!" the smiling woman exclaimed as ran to hug him.

Not waiting for the embrace to end, the man stepped up and hugged them both, the bluish essence of the Holy Spirit emanating from and entwining together with all three of them. "Your grandmother and I cannot tell you how excited we are that you are here!" the man finally said as the three of them stepped back to look at each other.

"I...I'm sorry," Milton stammered, "but I don't know you. Are you my mother's parents?"

"No, dear," the woman answered. "We are your father's parents. Our names are Michael and Trudy Tuttle."

"My father! I never knew who my father was. I don't even think my mother knew who he was. She just said that she lived a kind of wild life before I was born."

"Your father was wild and rebellious also," Michael added. "He left home as soon as he was old enough, and we never heard from him again…until we received word that he had died of an overdose."

"I'd love to meet him!" Milton said, looking around. "Is he here?"

"No, dear," Trudy said sadly, "he's not."

"We didn't know we had a grandson either," Michael said, "not until after our car wreck. That's when the angels brought us here."

"After we arrived, Jesus told us about you. Obviously we have been very interested in your life," Trudy said with a big smile.

"You were watching me?"

"Occasionally," Michael answered, "when Jesus saw you having special needs and difficult times, He wanted us to know so we could join Him in asking the Father to help you."

"Seriously! You were doing that…for me? But my life was such a mess!"

"To be honest, Milton," Michael said, "you did make some really bad decisions at times."

"Most of the time," Milton said humbly.

"But, Sweetheart, you had almost no help or support your whole life," Trudy consoled. "Jesus kept calling to you, but you were so absorbed with yourself that you just wouldn't listen."

"Not until my life fell apart," Milton admitted.

"It broke our hearts when Carol left you," Trudy said with feeling.

"It was the drugs, the alcohol, and the irresponsibility," said Milton. "She couldn't stay with me when I was into all that. Then when I lost my job because of it, I had nothing left."

"But all that is what it took for you to finally turn to Jesus, the Savior," Michael said.

"How are you feeling right now?" Trudy asked, looking at him closely.

"I know that what you're saying is true, but I feel so badly about the hurt I left behind me. I didn't have a chance to make it right with Carol."

"I thought you might feel that way," Trudy said as she pulled something out of the pocket of her robe. "Here, I've brought you these."

She held up three large, glossy leaves. When Milton took them from her hand, he noticed that they had a strong and unique fragrance. He also saw the Spirit of God swirling around the leaves.

"Those are leaves from the Tree of Life," Michael explained excitedly.

"The Tree of Life?" Milton questioned.

"Oh, yes," said Michael. "It's this gigantic tree that grows on both sides of the River of Life." His grandfather pointed to the dancing river flowing beside them. "The river flows right under the Tree of Life! It produces twelve different types of fruit that are delicious, I might add. Just wait till you see it!"

"But its leaves are for healing," Trudy said quickly. "That's why I brought them for you. Your heart needs healing."

"So what do I do with them?" Milton asked.

"Hold them close to your face and breathe in their fragrance."

As Milton did so, an amazing sense of peace and wellbeing flooded his spirit. A smile spread across his face as he continued inhaling the beautifully sweet smell of the leaves. "Wow, this is really something. I can see it now," Milton agreed. "As crazy as it sounds, I can clearly see that losing Carol and my job was the best thing that ever happened to me. I hate all the pain and trouble I caused her and everyone at work, but you're right, Michael, I never would have gotten here without going through all that.

"I was such a selfish fool," Milton continued, "but Jesus kept pursuing me. He took me where I was and used all my terrible choices to bring me to Him. My friend Scott was right! He is such an amazing King!"

"Oh, yes, He is!" Trudy agreed excitedly as she gave her grandson another hug.

"And the longer you are here," Michael added, "the more you will learn about the greatness of His love for us! He is constantly showing all of us something new and amazing about Himself. The things He shows us are so wonderful that you think your heart is going to burst with the joy you feel!"

"As soon as you come to grips with the amazing glory Jesus has displayed," Trudy said, "He reveals something even more stunning about Himself and the Father! It's so wonderful! You are going to love it here!"

Chapter Nine

Chapter Ten

The demon's claws pierced deeply into both of Miller's arms as the creature flew away with him. The pain was intense and, for the first time, brought Blake to the stunning realization that this nightmare was reality. The pain was real! The demons were real! And that meant hell was real, and he was about to be cast into it!

When the truth struck him, the fear it produced in him was immeasurable. An involuntary scream burst from the depths of his chest more from fear than the pain. In response, the demon laughed maniacally.

The formation of satanic creatures carried their victim over a dark hill, and immediately a wave of heat blasted Miller's face and arms. Below him he saw what appeared to be an ocean of fire. As they rushed onward, the demons dove toward the shore of the huge, flaming sea.

Chapter Ten

They landed beside a heavy metal structure with an iron beam attached. Shackles dangled from the end of the beam and were quickly snapped around Miller's wrists. The metal of the shackles was so hot that it blistered his wrists, and again Miller cried in pain. Once he was chained, the demons threw him over the edge and out toward the flames.

Blake's scream of terror was cut short when the shackles that held him stopped his fall with a painful jerk. He found himself swinging perilously above the fire as the demons shoved the beam further out and over the great, burning sea. The sulphur fumes stung his eyes and seared his nostrils. The intense heat started to blister his exposed skin. Below him he could see the heads and upper bodies of thousands and thousands of others, all screaming in torment.

Miller yelled for mercy, but his tormentors only laughed and threw rocks and dust at him. As Blake looked at the demons on the shore, he was terrified to see the boss pull out a wicked-looking black sword and, after giving his victim a fiendish grin, start chopping at Blake's silver life line.

Sparks flew when the blade hit the shimmery cord, but to Miller's great relief, it held. The pain from the iron shackles cutting into his wrists and the intense heat were overwhelming. All of this added to the terror of what awaited him if his severely injured self back at the plane crash died. It was too horrible to even imagine. Miller felt that he was going crazy.

One sane thought managed to force its way into his tormented mind, and it was that His faithful grandmother was praying to her King and Savior for him. Blake clung to that thought like a drowning man clings to a life preserver. He cried out with all his heart, "NANA! HELP ME! PLEASE, NANA, HELP ME!"

Miller's pathetic cries only resulted in more eruptions of cackling laughter from the gang of tormentors nearby. "Yer' Nana ain't gonna help you here, human!" the boss demon laughed.

Miller realized the truth of that hateful statement and decided to try something different. Something he had never done before in his life. "JESUS CHRIST!" the tortured young man screamed.

As soon as those two words left his lips, the demons went crazy. They roared their rage at their victim and began throwing more rocks and dust, trying to shut him up.

Coughing and spitting dust out of his mouth, Blake continued. "JESUS CHRIST! YOU

KNOW MY NANA…EDITH MILLER! SHE LOVES YOU A LOT, AND SHE'S PRAYING TO YOU RIGHT NOW FOR ME! PLEASE LISTEN TO HER, JESUS, AND HELP ME! I'M IN REALLY BIG TROUBLE!" As he finished those words, Blake broke down in deep sobs as more rocks and dirt hit him.

A few moments later a deep, resonating, bonging sound reverberated across the darkness. It was like the booming of an enormous gong. Even as he hung there, Blake felt the vibrations of it.

"WE'RE UNDER ATTACK!" the boss yelled to the others. "COME ON!" He held up his sword, yelled a war cry, and shot into the black sky. The other demons yanked out their weapons and followed, screaming as they flew.

Craning his neck and head around, in the far distance Blake could see what appeared to be an army of bright figures charging out of the city of light. "They're too far away to do me any good," Blake groaned in disappointment.

"How about us?" a familiar voice called from the shore.

At that moment the beam from which Blake hung was swung back around by Tirian and Barcos. As soon as they had Blake over the ground, Barcos used his powerful sword and broke the shackles holding him. Tirian caught Blake as he dropped, and the rescued young man clung desperately to the angel.

"Thank you for coming for me!" Blake sobbed. "Thank you! Thank you!"

"We're going to get you to a safe place," Tirian said with compassion.

Just as they were about to leave with Blake, a loud horn sounded nearby. Looking in the direction of the trumpet blast, they saw a demon a short distance away blowing an alarm.

"They left one to watch the prisoner!" Barcos yelled.

"We never saw him," Tirian declared. "He must have hid when he spotted us coming to save the human."

"He is calling all the demons back on us!" Barcos roared as he whipped out his long sword and flew like a rocket at the guard. As he charged past the enemy, his weapon slashed, and the guard collapsed with dark, steamy smoke pouring out of a large gash in his side.

Instantly Barcos was back with his companions. "Demons are rushing towards us!" the bronze giant announced urgently. "They'll be here quickly!"

"Hurry! Over those rocks!" Tirian ordered and launched into the air, tightly gripping the terrified Blake. The silver angel stayed close to the ground as they raced over and around the many large boulders littering the space in front of them. Barcos flew behind and to the side so that the wind from his wings blew dust and cinders over the silver cord trailing behind Blake.

As soon as they were out of sight of the sea of fire, Tirian turned sharply to his right and kept flying hard. A large mass of black rock loomed in front of them, and the angel whipped behind it with Barcos in his wake.

At that moment the fierce cries of a hundred demons pierced the darkness as the vengeful army poured past the hiding spot in pursuit of their stolen victim.

"That's a lot of demons," Barcos observed as they watched the screaming horde speed off into the darkness.

"We can't hide him near the crash site," Tirian returned. "With so many searching, they'll find us for sure."

"We need to go where they won't look," Barcos added.

"That means heading toward the Lair!" Tirian exclaimed.

"I don't like it either," Barcos said, "but we have no other choice. I will go first. You follow with him."

Cautiously, while staying in the dark shadows, they moved towards the demons' stronghold. Almost paralyzed with fear, Blake clung tightly to the silver angel. When Barcos came to the dark shadow of another large boulder, Tirian called for a halt. "Let's stop for a moment, Barcos. Our friend here needs help.

"Let me look at your wounds," Tirian said as he sat the terrified man down and began to examine the deep punctures from the demon's claws on Blake's arms. There was no blood coming from the wounds. Instead something like a steamy smoke leaked out of them. Blake noticed the smoke for the first time and panicked even more. "WHAT IS THAT COMING OUT OF MY ARMS?"

"It is your spiritual essence," Tirian answered calmly. "We don't have blood in the spirit world like you do in the land of shadows, the place you call earth. Deep wounds here cause loss of that essence. You won't die from it. That doesn't happen here. But you can lose enough of your essence to make you very weak." While he was speaking, the silver angel held his hand over

Blake's wounds. When he removed them, there appeared to be a bandage of light covering the punctures.

Even though the pain in his arms had lessened from the treatment, Blake was still emotionally distraught at the terrifying episode he had experienced with the demons. "This is real…THIS IS REAL…oh no, no, no, no…," Miller agonizingly repeated to himself as he rubbed his face and head with both hands.

"Blake Miller," Tirian spoke to the terrified man. When the angel got no response except for more repetitive mumbling, he tried again, touching Miller on the shoulder.

Suddenly Blake lunged at the angel, gripped his arms, and screamed, "THIS IS REAL! THIS IS REALLY REAL! WHAT AM I GONNA DO?"

Tirian reached up and pulled the panicking man's arms down. "The first thing you're going to do is calm down," the angel advised, "Barcos and I are going to help you but you must do what we tell you to do. Do you understand?"

Instead of answering, Blake's eyes shot all around, desperately searching for an escape from the terror of this ordeal.

Tirian quickly put his hands on either side of Miller's face to force him to look at the angel.

"BLAKE MILLER, YOU MUST CALM DOWN AND DO WHAT WE SAY! DO YOU UNDERSTAND?"

"Okay…okay!" Blake managed to get out. "Yes…understand!"

"The Master heard your cry and your grandmother's prayers," Tirian explained. "He sent the host to attack the Demons' Lair as a distraction to allow Barcos and me to slip back and rescue you. Because you cried out to Him, the Master is going to help you."

Blake seemed to comprehend the angel's words. He stared into Tirian's eyes and saw a look that communicated determination, loyalty, and truth. The distressed young man realized that, if help could be found in this God-forsaken place, these two would do all in their power to aid him.

Since Miller's wounds were taken care of, Barcos led them from their place of concealment. He eventually came to a large, jagged boulder. Hiding in the large rock's dark shadow, Barcos pointed across a wide, open area to a jagged black crag. "The Lair," he announced in a low voice.

In response to the declaration, Blake Miller stole a look at the evil place, and his shaking got worse. Before them was a small, porous-looking mountain. The multiple, cave-like openings all over its surface made it look like a giant, black sponge. Frequently demons could be seen darting in and out of the many openings in its side.

"We sh...shouldn't be here!" he stuttered in horror.

"No, we shouldn't," Tirian hissed back, "but right now we've no place else to go where we won't be found."

Just then screaming and yelling was heard behind them. "Demons come!" Barcos warned as he looked back the way they had traveled. "They will find us here!"

"Please don't let them catch me!" Blake exclaimed with a wild look in his eyes.

Both of the angels frantically searched their surroundings. Finally Barcos made a decision. "Come!" he said and rushed quickly toward the Demons' Lair.

"NO! NO!" Miller cried in a panic when he saw where they were headed. Immediately Tirian's hand tightly covered his mouth. With three flaps of their powerful wings, the two angels shot into the closest opening in the enemy's fortress.

"This is insane, Barcos!" Tirian hissed as they stood in the tall, dark opening.

"Yes," the giant agreed. "Be silent."

Suddenly there was a loud flapping of wings, and a group of six demons landed just in the front of the same cave opening.

"That was a pitiful attack," an evil voice sneered. "We drove the clowns of light back handily this time! Either they are getting weaker, or we are getting stronger!"

"Maybe both, my Ba-al," another demon answered with a sneering laugh.

"Even so," the chief returned, "double the watchers so they can't surprise us again, then send the rest of my command back to harvesting souls."

"It will be done," came the subservient answer.

Barcos reached over and touched Tirian on the shoulder and gave an urgent signal that they should move further into the passageway. His companion nodded his understanding.

Assured that his orders would be carried out, the demon commander spun around and strutted down the tall, dark passageway and toward the retreating angels.

Barcos sensed the approaching enemy and led the other two rapidly along the murky corridor. They rushed forward silently, not knowing where they were going. The place smelled like rot and death, but the thought of what would happen to them if they were caught made that insignificant.

The passage widened but was still quite dark, lit only by the dim glow of occasional red crystals resting on rock ledges. The walls were not smooth but rather rough and jagged, like the rock had been chipped or blasted away. Just ahead was a larger room lit by flickering flames. As Barcos started to enter the room, he sensed the presence of enemies and slid to a halt. Peeking around the corner, he saw several demon commanders arguing with each other.

"Back! Back!" the bronze giant hissed urgently and pushed his friends away from the opening.

Chapter Eleven

As Tirian, Barcos, and Blake turned and retraced their way through the dark passage in the Demons' Lair, they suddenly heard the approaching footfalls of the enemy leader they had been running from. In panic, the angels slid to a stop and frantically searched for a place to hide. Three seconds later the commander strode into the dark anti-chamber. A faint noise nearby caused him to pause and listen suspiciously, but just then the voices of the arguing commanders in the next room broke the silence, and he quickly passed into the lighted chamber with the other leaders.

Once he was gone, what appeared to be two large, protruding rocks near the ceiling shifted so that each of the angels who had been covered by their wings could view the room below them.

"Let's try to leave while we can," Tirian whispered to his friend.

"No!" the giant hissed back. "The demons are too close. If we make any noise, we are caught. Stay here for now."

The argument between the evil commanders grew loud, and their voices carried to the three who were hidden around the corner.

"I'm telling you, Ba-al Rabog," one of the voices snarled, "it's becoming a pattern! More and more of the souls that enter through the veil are being taken by the angels—which means that more shadowlanders are seeing through our master's lies. They are escaping our traps and believing the Holy One's words." As soon as he mentioned the Holy One, all of the demons snarled or spat.

"Is the increase in the number of those escaping happening all over the world?" Rabog asked with concern.

"No, thank Lucifer," the answer came back. "The princes of America, Canada, and Europe seem to have effective control of their territories. But when the prince of Persia and the prince of Asia hear these reports they are going to be furious. For hundreds of years their territories have been locked up, completely controlled by our great master's deceptions. No light has been able to get past those walls of darkness!"

"What are you saying?" Rabog demanded. "Are the fortifications of the Great Nations of Lucifer weakening?"

"They are not just weakening, Ba-al. They are collapsing!"

"WHAT?" Rabog screamed. "That can't be! It's impossible! The reports must be lies!"

"I wish it were so," the demon commander answered sorrowfully, "but my overseers insist that the reports are true! They say that as the souls of the dead come through the veil from those territories, many are delivered from our demons by the angels."

"And you believe this report, Miragash?"

"I have been among my harvesters and have seen it myself!" Ba-al Miragash huffed, chaffing at his report being questioned.

"What is happening?" Rabog demanded. "How could this calamity occur in the very heart of our master's kingdom?"

"Obviously the princes are becoming fat and lazy," Miragash answered out of the side of his mouth in a low voice as he scanned the room for spies. "Like you, I have no idea what's happening in the land of shadows. I only see the results as they appear on this side of the veil, and what I see doesn't look good."

There was silence in the room for several long moments. Finally Rabog voiced his opinion. "You are right, Miragash. The princes must be told, but I don't want to be around when you inform them."

"Neither do I!" Miragash returned with a scared look. "Maybe I'll have my sub-commander do it. He's been trying to get my position for some time. When the princes hear what's happening, they will be so furious that they'll probably slash him to ribbons."

"This is a terrible disaster, Rabog!" Jarmuth, another demon commander said, joining the discussion. "Something like this hasn't happened in the Persian territory for almost two thousand years. We have all heard the great prince brag about how secure his principality is."

"How do you think the big shots will handle this, Rabog?" Miragash wondered.

"Our master has such a strong hold on the North American principalities," Rabog said his thoughts out loud, "that it would be logical to send some of our forces to the weakening areas to crush any spread of the light."

"Do they dare weaken the forces in North America?" Jarmuth questioned. "We could lose even more territory!"

"It shouldn't be a problem," Rabog continued. "Those selfish human creatures there are so consumed with their own pleasures that there's really not that much work for the demons to do.

"Even their churches are so separated and self-absorbed that they will never be able to unite against us. They don't even think about us; they're too busy squabbling and competing against each other. Besides, our master has many of the religious leaders firmly in his pocket."

"How so?" Jarmuth questioned with interest.

"Many of the religious leaders are only interested in control over their churches. The arrogance in some of them is enormous, and it only takes the infusion of a little bit of pride for them to be susceptible to our master's influence.

"Great numbers of the church leaders have given up using the holy book altogether, except when it suits them. When broken shadowlanders come to them wanting salvation, they are told to do things that aren't even in the Creator's book, and nobody seems to care."

Jarmuth laughed, "Those fools wind up following deluded religious leaders or man-made groups rather than the Holy One." When this name was mentioned again, the rest spat or snarled.

"Hopefully that's the way it is," Miragash said, inserting himself back into the conversation. "But the last time our leaders came for their reports, I remember hearing the great prince over Persia berating the prince of America for getting slack and letting pockets of resistance build up against the darkness."

"It's those repulsive praying believers," Rabog snarled. "You think you've got them satisfied and complacent, and then a few of the slimy weasels slip free and get the disgusting idea of praying. It makes me sick to my stomach just to think about it! Some of them even start praying TOGETHER! That's when things really start getting messed up!"

"Yes," Jarmuth agreed, "it's terrifying how much damage even a few of those people praying together can do to the work. I hate them! We send the demons against them, but when those dimwits figure out what we're doing, then they start praying against US! That's when it ALL begins falling apart!

"I know about this stuff, Rabog! That actually happened to me in the last assignment I had before I got sent here. It was awful!"

"If the princes are going to pull forces out of North America," Miragash stated, "they better stir things up there first to keep the shadowlanders at each other's throats, or maybe start an epidemic of lust, self-centeredness, and pleasure-craving like they did back in the twenties and the sixties—anything to keep them obsessing over themselves rather than praying!"

"I see your point, Miragash," Rabog admitted. "Unfortunately the princes are so arrogant, they'd never listen to any advice."

"Well, if the princes don't figure this out quickly," Miragash snarled back, "Lucifer will start adding THEM to his collection!"

"Keep your voice down!" Jarmuth hissed. "You know they all have their spies here! I don't know about you two, but I've been demoted enough!"

"BA-AL RABOG!"

Both hiding angels flinched. The shout had come from the dark tunnel behind them. Closing their wings and resuming the appearance of the rocks, the heavenly guardians tensed for the passing of more demons.

"BA-AL RABOG!" the voice shouted again and was followed by the sound of approaching footsteps.

"What is it?" Rabog snapped irritably as he stepped into the long, dark hall and confronted the messenger directly below the hiding angels.

"The brigade you sent out has been unable to find the escaped prisoner."

"WHAT?" the demon commander screamed. "IS EVERY ONE OF YOU TOTALLY INCOMPETENT?"

"But, my Ba-al," the messenger began defensively, "we thoroughly searched the area and…"

"YOU ABSOLUTE FOOLS!" Rabog screamed again. "HE HAS A LIFELINE! Go back to the injured body AND FOLLOW IT! He couldn't be hiding from you if he didn't have help from some angels! I WANT THEM TOO!"

As the messenger raced out of the tunnel, Rabog stuck his head back into the lit room and spoke to the other commanders.

"Would you two send some of your troops to help us find this escaped prisoner?" The response he got was growls. "If you catch him, you can have any angels helping him."

Evil grins spread across both of their wicked faces as they rose from their seats and walked purposefully past Rabog and up the dark exit tunnel.

As Rabog started to follow them, something caught his eye. Coming out of the black cinders covering the floor was a very thin, shimmery cord. It ran in between some of the jagged crevasses in the wall and into a large, rocky protrusion hanging from the ceiling. Drawing his black sword, Rabog slowly extended the tip to poke the bulging rock.

Suddenly the large, rocky protrusion beside it exploded as Barcos dropped on top of the demon. With a swift slash, a large cloud of black smoke streamed from a massive gash in the evil commander's chest. Rabog lay on the floor with spiritual essence boiling out of him, too weak to move or speak.

"So what do we do now?" Tirian hissed as he too dropped to the floor with Blake.

"Rabog!" a voice called from the entrance of the tunnel.

Quickly Barcos snatched up the deflated Ba-al and hid his quivering form behind some large rocks.

"There are too many demons that way!" Barcos said, pointing toward the entrance. "None of us are going to like this but the way I see it , the only option we have is to move deeper into the Lair!"

Blake, with terror-filled eyes and with Tirian's large hand still covering his mouth, tried to shake his head *no*.

"Do other angels have to run around in the Demons' Lair?" Tirian asked in irritably.

"They are coming!" Barcos snapped, ignoring his companion's comment.

"What a mess!" Tirian shot back as they flew past the lit room and deeper into the bowels of the demon stronghold while Blake Miller emitted a muffled sob.

Chapter Twelve

As Barcos led the way along the dark tunnel, he held up a finger, and a golden light glowing from the tip illuminated their path. The bronze giant hurried to keep ahead of any demons coming from behind, yet he did so with cautious apprehension. This place was filled with enemies, and he did not want to run into any of them if he could help it.

The further they went, the clearer it became that the path was ascending. They came to openings that led into several dark rooms. Barcos paused long enough at the doorways of each one to make sure there were no enemies within.

Loud, snarling voices alerted them as they approached another opening. Flickering light coming from the room revealed its location before the angels arrived.

Drawing near to the edge of the entrance, Barcos snuck a peek inside. Slipping back to his friends, he whispered, "It's a barracks...many demons inside. There is a space between the top of the entrance and the ceiling. We will fly over the doorway."

Soundlessly the two angles glided over and further down the tunnel carrying their charge. They had only traveled a short distance when the passageway suddenly opened into a gigantic cavern. Large, glowing red crystals rested on various stone shelves and on the tops of rock columns, dimly illuminating the vast, open area.

Barcos and Tirian hid in the deep shadow of a large boulder as they strained to hear any sound that would indicate the presence of enemies in the vast room.

"P...please get me out of this horrible place!" Blake whispered in terror.

"We are trying, Blake Miller," Tirian answered. "But we are surrounded by a host of demons, and we must be careful!"

Tirian turned to Barcos and whispered, "If you do not detect any enemies, let's try finding a way out of here."

The bronze giant nodded his agreement and began cautiously moving from shadow to shadow across the large, open room. They had made it almost half way to the other side when, to their right, they heard a weak cry of fear.

Whipping out his sword and using his finger tip again, Barcos illuminated the dark shadows near them. He spotted a very weak-looking demon cowering in the dark.

"Angels!" the demon squeaked in terror. "You aren't supposed to be here!"

"Yeah, we know," Barcos returned as he examined the collapsed creature in front of him.

"Please don't hurt me!" the pitiful figure pleaded.

"We won't harm you if you don't give us a reason to," Tirian assured him. "What happened to you?"

"My master got mad at me," the demon whined, "and slashed me. I managed to drag myself in here to hide until I recovered enough of my essence so I could get my strength back."

"Is there a way out of here?" Barcos asked bluntly.

"Of course there's a way out of here, stupid!" the demon snapped.

"Now I know why you got slashed," the bronze giant observed. "Show us the way out."

"YOU'RE ANGELS! WHY SHOULD I?"

Barcos's sword hovered threateningly over the demonic creature. "Because it's going to take you much longer to recover your essence if you don't."

"Hey, you're angels!" the demon countered with a sneer. "You can't lie. The other angel said that you wouldn't hurt me."

"It is true that my angel friend and the shadowlander won't hurt you," Barcos returned without withdrawing his sword, "but I didn't promise anything, and I *will* hurt you. Now — which way out?"

Suddenly the creature's eyes grew wide, and he began trembling.

"SPEAK UP! Which way out?"

The terrified demon extended a trembling arm and pointed toward the far end of the great cavern. "There! The way out is over there!"

Barcos reached down and, with little effort, snatched up the disgusting figure. "Show us," he ordered.

The injured demon was too weak to resist but thrashed and whimpered in the angel's vice-like grip.

"Curse you, darkhater! Curse you!" he squeaked as he was carried forcefully across the room.

When they reached the other side, they discovered not one but two different passages. Barcos stood in both of them but could detect no light except the faint glow of the occasional red crystal. He tried to sense air movement, but there was none from either tunnel.

"Which one?" he demanded, shaking the demon.

"Guess!" the evil creature sneered and then gave a high, crackly laugh.

Barcos placed the razor-sharp edge of his sword against the throat of the demon. "I'm asking nicely," he growled as he pressed the blade until it began to bite into the creature's scaly skin. "Which one?"

The demon hesitated only a moment and then blurted out, "THE LEFT ONE!"

Barcos lifted his prisoner until he was looking directly into the demon's yellow eyes. After several moments he released the captive and announced, "We go right."

Still hissing curses, the terrified enemy hurriedly crawled away. As he did so, the giant bronze angel lit his finger tip and led his friends into the right passageway.

They moved cautiously along, twice having to negotiate past rooms containing off-duty demons. The tension was palpable, and all three of them knew that discovery by the enemy was almost inevitable. Barcos continued along the dimly lit passageway for several minutes, then suddenly stopped. Turning to the others, he whispered, "I feel a slight breeze."

"I feel it too," Tirian whispered back. "We must be near an exit."

Unexpectedly, loud voices were heard just ahead of them.

"Demons!" Barcos warned. "Hide on the ceiling again."

As Tirian leaped up and gripped the jagged rocks above them, Barcos grabbed the nearest glowing crystals and threw them back down the tunnel the way they had come. With the passageway now engulfed in darkness, Barcos joined Tirian on the ceiling. They pulled their wings tightly around them just as the marching company of demons arrived.

Blake was beside himself with fear, and the silver angel slipped his free hand over the shadowlander's mouth once more. The two angels held perfectly still as over thirty enemy warriors passed below them, close enough to touch.

All sounds of their passing had trailed off when Barcos parted his wings to take a look.

Finally he whispered to his companion, "I'll scout it out."

It was almost five minutes later when the huge angel returned. "The exit is just up ahead," he whispered, "but there are many demons positioned there."

"Do we wait till they leave?" Tirian asked.

"It appears to be a staging area for sending out their squads," Barcos returned. "It looks to me that demons in numbers are always posted there."

"Should we go back in and try to find another way?"

"Oh, please, no!" Blake whimpered.

"*Shhhhh!*" Tirian hissed, trying to quiet him. "What do you think would be our best move, Barcos?"

The bronze giant thought for several long moments. Finally he spoke. "We can't stay here. With all the demons coming and from this place, they will surely discover us. I also think returning into that hive of wickedness increases our chances of being caught. I don't like it but, given the danger of our situation, I think the best option is to exit here."

"You mean fight our way out?"

"No," Barcos returned. "We'd never make it, and if we did, we would be running away with the entire army after us. There would be no escape."

"So what do we do?"

"You hide here with the shadowlander, and I will draw the demons after me. Once they are all pursuing me, you slip out and take him back to the cave we found in order to give the Master time to do what He can for this one, or until his body dies. That is all we can do."

"Let me do it, Barcos," Tirian pleaded. "You take Blake Miller."

The huge angel placed his massive hand on his comrade's silver shoulder. "No, friend, I must do this. I am the strong one, and I can be more frightening. That you know."

"Yes, I have seen you in fierce battle, and there is none who can stand before you."

"So I will lead them away from here," Barcos said again, "while you, being faster and quite clever, will slip away unnoticed to a safe hiding place for the shadowlander."

"I will do it," Tirian agreed, "but I am very concerned for you."

"I am convinced it is what our Master would want us to do. Stay back in the darkness until after I lead them off before you come out, and then fly as fast as you can away from here."

"I will," the silver angel acknowledged. "Our all-powerful Master be with you, my good friend."

"And with you," Barcos said as they gripped each other's forearms firmly.

Turning toward the opening, Barcos began to creep silently to the exit. He stood in the shadows, studying the position of the enemy troops. Finally he took a deep breath, stood up to his full height, and let out a bellowing roar that could be heard a league away. "FOR THE LORD JESUS CHRIST!"

Both the loud roar as well as the unmentionable name of the One they feared the most sent all of the demons racing for cover.

Suddenly the giant bronze angel began to radiate a brilliant light that burned the eyes of those who tried to look at him. Then he launched into the air and flew rapidly away to the left across the face of the entire lair.

Realizing that it was only one angel that opposed them, every demon present screamed their rage and charged after him.

Several moments later Tirian stepped cautiously from the opening and, seeing no enemies, shot away in the opposite direction with Blake Miller. Glancing over his left shoulder as he flew, he saw in the distance a brilliant point of light being rapidly pursued by what appeared to be an enormous, angry black cloud.

"Oh, Master, help him!" Tirian said as he raced in the opposite direction.

Chapter Thirteen

Milton, Michael, and Trudy were standing near the great Tree of Life watching the rushing river flow under its wide roots when Jesus joined them.

"How do you like having a family?" the King asked the new citizen of Paradise.

"I love them!" Milton exclaimed, reaching across both of their shoulders to hug Michael and Trudy as the presence of the Spirit of God swirled lovingly around them. "But, You know, it's hard to think of them as my grandparents since everybody here looks to be about the same age. They've been telling me so much about their lives on earth that I missed and about this wonderful place."

"We thought we'd show him some of the beauties of Paradise, Your Majesty," Michael explained, "but every time we pass a group of the brothers and sisters who are singing praises, Milton wants to stop."

"I was never able to sing on earth," Milton said, "but I can here! It's amazing! I sound as good as the others!"

"It lifts your heart to sing well, doesn't it?" Jesus asked him with a knowing smile.

"You know," Milton answered in amazement, "it really does! I used to enjoy the singers at the church where Scott and his friends would go, but as good as they were, it was nothing like this!"

"All of that was just shadows, My friend," Jesus explained. "It saddens Me to say, but even the churches and their worship are deeply touched by the darkness there.

"Come with Me, the three of you," Jesus invited. "I want to show you what I mean."

The King led his friends around the left side of a gorgeously manicured garden where there was a large building with dark green walls made of pure jade. They entered a long hallway with a vast ceiling. Bands of gold inlaid the rich stone walls. Huge arched windows reaching almost from the floor to the ceiling of the vast hallway. The windows were like the massive stained glass ones they had seen in pictures of European cathedrals, but these were much more beautiful. They were stunningly detailed and intricate.

When Milton asked about the stained glass windows, Jesus revealed that there was no glass in them. All of the colored and clear panes were made of thin sheets of precious stones and held in place with gold.

"You mean even the clear panes aren't glass?" Milton asked in amazement.

"Diamond sheets," Jesus smiled back.

Milton wanted to stay and admire each one, but, firmly, Jesus kept them walking. At last they came to a set of beautifully carved, double doors made of gold and inlaid with silver.

"Where are we, Master?" Trudy asked. "I've never been here."

"This is the World Room of Lampstands," Jesus answered soberly. "I actually come here often. But I must warn you: there is both joy and sadness in this place."

"Sadness?" Trudy asked with surprise. "Here?"

"You will see," the King answered with a sigh.

As Jesus stepped in front of the large doors, they opened of their own accord. The room had no windows but there was a golden, defused glow emanating from the walls and the ceiling. It created a solemn atmosphere. The Spirit of God flowed around them as the three friends of Jesus stepped into the vast room. They noticed that the floor was a large, colored map of the entire world as they had known it. Scattered over the surface of the map were thousands of burning lampstands, each with seven lamps like a Jewish menorah. The light shining from a few was so brilliant that it was difficult to look at them. Most were much dimmer. A few were barely producing any light at all. The brightest ones were located in the part of the large map that represented the Middle East.

"What is all this, Your Majesty?" Milton asked what the others were wondering.

"This room is one of the ways I keep up with My followers. By viewing the lampstands here, I can see instantly who has allowed My Spirit to fill them and whose faith is failing."

"Master, ever since I became a believer in You," Milton voiced eagerly, "I wanted to be filled with more and more of your Spirit, but I never could figure out how to do it. My friends and I used to talk about that a lot, wondering what a person had to do to get more of the Holy Spirit."

"Friends," Jesus answered, "the Spirit of Truth is not a thing. He is an amazing and wonderful person. When He comes into your life , He doesn't just send a part of Himself. When you receive My Spirit, you receive *all* of Him. It is not a matter of how much of the Holy Spirit that you receive. It is all about how much of *you* the Holy Spirit gets. If a person wants to be filled with My Spirit, it is simply a matter of welcoming Him into every nook and cranny of their life."

"You said this room can tell You what's happening in the lives of Your followers on earth," Michael said. "How do these lamps tell You that?"

"Come with Me," Jesus said and walked across the mapped floor, weaving around the many lampstands. He came to the place that represented the United States and stood over the spot where Milton's town would have been. There were several lampstands in this area.

"Each of these lampstands represents a group of My followers. You would call them a church." Jesus pointed to one stand in particular and said, "Milton, the church you were a part of with Scott and his wife is represented by this stand."

"What's wrong with it, Lord?" Milton asked as he stared at the stand in confusion. "Two of the seven lamps are out, four are barely burning at all, and only one is burning brightly."

"Sadly," Jesus began, "many of the people who attend there are no longer seeking Me. They have substituted loving their religion and their group for loving Me, and there is no light in them. They have let their passion and zeal for Me go out. Other people there are being influenced by them and are quickly becoming like them.

"My servant Scott, his wife, Phyllis, and a few others are letting My love shine brightly through their lives, but they are few in number. Losing you, Milton, has been a heavy blow to them."

"I don't want them to grieve for me, Your Majesty. I'm here because of them! Can you help them through the sadness and loss caused by my death?" Milton asked with concern. "Would you please encourage them and let them know that I'm doing great here?"

"Thank you for asking that for them," the King smiled in response. "Yes, I will. I will also send blessings to encourage them, as well as a rebuke and a challenge to the others."

Suddenly a heavenly messenger appeared, bowing before Jesus. "You sent for me, Master?"

Jesus placed His hand on the lampstand beside Him and said, "To those who speak for Me at Louisburg, tell them that the One Who called them and Who loves them best says this: 'I know your deeds. A few of you have held faithfully to My words and are showing My love to others. Receive My comfort in the loss of My faithful servant, Milton Collins. Continue in your faithfulness to Me and you will also receive the blessings and delights that Milton enjoys now. Be blessed and encouraged, for the fire you have for Me burns brightly in you.'

Jesus continued with His message, "Many others in your church seem active and busy but really they are dead. Their light has gone out, and their religion is a burden to Me. Give these words of Mine to them: 'Turn from the path you are on. Let those who burn brightly for Me share their fire with you, and rekindle the flaming love you once had for Me. If you reject the spirit of My faithful ones, I will reject you. He who is still able to hear My words, let him hear.'"

When Jesus finished, the Holy Spirit flowed into the angel. The divine messenger bowed again and shot away to deliver the King's message.

"Your Majesty," Michael observed solemnly, "I can see a few of the lampstands that have gone completely out."

"If you look closely," Jesus answered, "you will see that, in some of those lamps, the wicks still smolder. There remains hope for them, and I have not abandoned them. I will continue to communicate My heart to the people there, but they are in deep trouble.

The lampstands that have completely gone out represent churches that no longer worship, serve, or follow Me, and My Spirit is no longer welcome there. They have their activities, their programs, and their religious busy work, but it is all done for themselves…to enlarge their group. They are no longer alive to Me. Those lampstands will be removed." Jesus pointed out a cold, dark lampstand that Michael had spotted.

Suddenly another angel appeared, and Jesus nodded toward the dark stand. The angel bowed to the Master, then picked up the dead lamp and carried it out of the room. Jesus indicated to the others that they should follow.

There was a small doorway in the side wall of the great room. The door opened as the angel carrying the lampstand approached it. Jesus led His three friends through the door, following the angel.

They walked onto a wide, stone porch. The angel carried the dead lamp to the end of the porch and threw it off. When Jesus led them to the edge, Milton and the others look down into a deep pit, the bottom of which was covered with thousands of broken lampstands.

As they stared forlornly at the bottom of the pit, Jesus sighed and said, "That, my dear friends, is the saddest sight in all of Paradise."

Chapter Thirteen

Chapter Fourteen

Tirian flew as fast as he could. The ground passing rapidly below them was a blur to Blake Miller. A short flight brought them back to the cave where they had first hidden. He gently placed Blake on the dirty floor and returned to the cave entrance where the angel intensely combed the sky for any sign of enemy search parties.

Tirian turned and stood in front of Miller. "There doesn't appear to be any danger for now," Tirian began. "I must leave for a few moments to cover your silver cord so that the demons cannot track us here, but I will return quickly."

Blake Miller seemed not to hear the angel's words, and Tirian noticed that he was not doing well. The young man sat in the back of the cave with his knees pulled up to his chest and his arms wrapped tightly around them. He rocked back and forth, whimpering to himself.

With a sigh the silver angel flew out of the cave. He sped near the ground, following the flickering life line. The wind from his wings as he zipped past stirred enough dust and cinders to hide the cord from view. He covered as much territory as he dared. Occasionally he heard voices nearby and hid himself in the dark shadows of the rocks and boulders. When he felt the risk was least, he made a rapid break for the cave.

After he returned, the silver-skinned angel once again posted himself by the cave opening, examining the darkness for any evidence of the searching demons. Satisfied that they were safe for the moment, Tirian went back to check on Miller. What the angel saw disturbed him. He studied the terrified and overwhelmed young human before him. Seldom had he seen a person from the land of shadows who was so utterly horrified and crushed in spirit as this man.

"You are safe now," the angel said, trying to ease the stress of the pitiful creature.

When he got no response, the angel tried again. "Did you hear me? I said you are safe. Barcos is leading our enemies away from us, and I have brought you back to the cave. The demons will not likely find us here. There is no reason for you to be so terrified."

Again the only response was more mindless rocking, trembling, and anxious mumbling. Tirian didn't know a lot about how the human mind worked, but he understood enough to realize that, if this one continued in his present state, he would soon go insane. That's something that the angel had seen before, so he attempted once again to draw the petrified human back to a place of reason.

"Try to listen to me," the angel said as he gripped the young man's forearm. "What you're doing isn't helping."

Blake stopped his rocking and looked straight at the silver angel, but the severe trembling didn't stop.

"You should try to calm down, Blake Miller," Tirian said.

"C...calm down! How do I calm down? Look at what's happened to me! I...I...I've been attacked by demons...REAL DEMONS!"

Tirian nodded his head in calm agreement.

"I...I've been chained up and dangled over hell...REAL HELL! I didn't believe any of this existed. And now, when it's too late, I find out that IT DOES! And you want me to calm down? How do I do that? It's too late to calm down...too late!"

"It may not be too late, Blake Miller," Tirian returned. "You haven't died yet. There may yet be hope. Our Master said that He would help you."

"He already did!" Blake shot back. "He sent the emergency people, but the demons ran them off before they could find me! They were my only chance of being rescued. You saw how badly injured my body is. There's no way I can last much longer! I'm surprised I'm not already dead! There is no hope for me! NONE! I'm as good as thrown in that pit of fire to wait in torment for a judgment, and I already know the verdict! I've been a terrible person and have rejected and cursed your Master all my life. How can I calm down when I know my awful future?" Once again Blake began rocking back and forth and moaning in terror.

Tirian thought for a moment, then reached out and grabbed Miller's arm once more. "You should calm down because our Master has promised to work for you."

"That's an empty promise!" Blake snapped in exasperation. "What can He possibly do? Don't you understand? Now that the emergency people are gone, nobody's looking for me. And even if they were, the police won't let anyone into a dangerous crash site. With my severe injuries, you know as well as I do that I'll be dead soon. What can He do?"

"Our Master can do anything," the silver angel answered firmly and confidently. "If you knew Him, you would not be so upset. You would calmly trust Him, even in what looks like an impossible situation."

"Oh, that's easy for you to say!" Blake barked angrily. "You're not the one sitting here holding a ticket to hell!"

"Let me tell you a true story, Blake Miller," the angel began. "Many of your years ago, my Master had three followers who were forced to serve a cruel king, which they faithfully did as his wise men. Eventually the king made a huge golden image, an idol, and he commanded everyone in his great kingdom to bow down and worship it or be thrown into a fiery furnace."

"Well, that's one way to get converts," Blake sneered sarcastically.

"When the day came, everyone bowed down to the king's image," Tirian continued, "everyone except my Master's followers. To honor my Master they refused."

"You know, for wise men, that was about the dumbest decision those guys could make," Blake spoke his thoughts.

"That is not the way my Master's three followers saw it," said Tirian. "They were faithful to my Master and refused to worship anyone but Him. They told the king that, because they were followers of my Master, they were unable to worship the king's idol. When the king threatened to throw them into the furnace, they said that their Master was able to save them from the fire, but, even if He didn't, they would not be unfaithful to Him."

"Well, how'd that go for them?" Blake asked skeptically.

"The king was angry with them and commanded that the furnace be heated seven times hotter than normal. Then he ordered that the three followers of my Master to be bound and thrown into the raging fire, which was immediately done. It was so hot that even the soldiers who threw them in were immediately consumed by the flames."

"SEE? THAT'S WHAT I'M TALKING ABOUT!" Blake shot back in a panic. "If your Master couldn't deliver His faithful followers, what's He going to do for me?

"This is a terrible story! I can't believe you thought that would help me! If you're trying to encourage me, you've failed miserably!"

"But that is not the end of it, Blake Miller."

"What do you mean, 'it's not the end'?" Miller questioned in frustration. "Of course it is! They got thrown into the huge fire. Even the soldiers throwing them in got burned up. Everybody dies! End of story! END OF BLAKE MILLER!"

"Can I finish now?" Tirian asked.

"The king got as close to the opening of the blazing furnace as he could, and when he looked inside, he saw four people walking around in the flames unharmed."

"Four people? ALIVE?"

"Yes," Tirian answered. "He recognized the three he had condemned, but when he looked at the fourth on who was with them, the king said that He looked like a son of God."

"A son of God?" Blake asked with surprise.

"My Master!" Tirian said proudly. "Nothing is too hard for Him. No task is impossible for Him. He knows all things, has all power, and always accomplishes His will! If My Master wants you rescued, Blake Miller, He will do it, and there is nothing the demons or you or I can do to stop Him!"

"You know, you'd make a great salesman," Miller admitted. "I wish I had your faith."

"It is not faith with me," Tirian answered. "I know all of this is true because I have seen these things. The Master is not trying to grow faith in me. He is trying to grow it in you."

"What do you mean?" Miller asked.

"Who do you think kept you from dying in the plane crash when everyone else perished?" the silver angel probed.

"You're saying Jesus did that?" Miller questioned, genuinely puzzled. "Why? I'm as bad as the others. It makes no sense for Him to save me."

"Unless He wanted to honor your grandmother's faithful prayers," Tirian returned, "and because He loves you, and in His infinite wisdom, He wanted to give you a second chance to experience His love, even though you don't deserve it."

"I still don't get it," Blake said. "Why spare me? What could I possibly do for Him that would be worth all this effort to save my life?"

"This isn't about what you can do for Him," Tirian answered. "This is about Him showing you what He can do for you. My Master has an amazing love for you shadowlanders. I can't explain it. The other angels and I have talked about it, and it makes no sense to us. It is quite simply His holy nature to love all of you, and His love doesn't stop even when you do awful things to Him."

"That doesn't make sense!" Blake snapped. "What about that pit of fire over there? If He loves us so much, why does he let so many people get thrown in there?"

"How do you wake up every morning?" Tirian asked.

"What?"

"How do you wake up?" the angel persisted.

"I have an alarm set on my phone that wakes me up when it goes off. Why are you asking that?"

"What if you set your alarm to say *I love you* every morning?" Tirian asked. "Would you believe it?"

"No, of course not. It's just a machine."

"My Master doesn't want machines either," Tirian explained. "Love can only be genuine if it is a choice. That means you shadowlanders have the choice to either love my Master or to reject Him. Those who choose to love my Master, He blesses and takes to Paradise to be with Him. Those who choose not to love Him, He allows to have what they want…but it leads to hell."

Chapter Fourteen

Chapter Fifteen

As the silver stood by the cave entrance studying the dark angel sky and the surrounding shadows for signs of the search parties of demons, Blake Miller sat in the darkness contemplating what he had recently experienced and all the angel had told him. Glancing down, the young man saw his glowing lifeline. Miller picked it up and fingered the delicate-looking, shimmery cord between his fingers. That tiny thing represented the only hope he had for escaping the horrible torment he had just experienced. The more he thought about his predicament, the more depressed he became. "Tirian," he finally called.

"Yes."

"If I survive this whole ordeal and get back to earth, I would like for my life to be different. I really would! But there's no way! I've been thinking about it, and there is just no way! I know me, and I know I can't change! I'm just a bad person.

"You know there are some good people in the world...like my Nana. And there are bad people. I'm one of the bad ones. I always have been, and I always will be. I can't be good; it's just not in me!"

Tirian listened to Blake's hopeless summation of his life stoically. When the young man finished, the angel heard soft crying coming from the darkness.

Finally the holy guardian turned to face the sorrowful shadowlander. "Blake Miller," he began, "I told you before. This is not about what you can or cannot do. This is about what my Master can do."

"DON'T YOU GET IT?" Blake snapped. "It IS about me! I'm sure your Master is wonderful. My Nana certainly thinks so. I will even admit it: Jesus Christ is wonderful! BUT I AM NOT! I'm a terrible person!"

"That doesn't matter," Tirian returned.

"YES, IT DOES!" Blake argued. "I'M NOT GOOD ENOUGH TO BE ONE OF HIS FOLLOWERS!"

"No one is, Blake Miller—not even Lady Edith, your Nana. My Master said in His holy book that all have sinned and fallen short of the glory of God. All means all...you, Lady Edith, everyone. From the beginning my Master made all of you shadowlanders with limits and weaknesses. That's why He made you out of clay.

"He made us with weaknesses!" Blake snapped. "Why...so we would intentionally mess up our lives? Is He sadistic or something?"

"He made you weak, Blake Miller, so you would realize how much you need Him. It is only when a person gets to the place where they realize that they desperately need help that they will turn to my Master. What you don't realize is how powerful my Master is.

"When He came to your earth, the place of shadows, He came to show each of you what *good enough* looked like. Then He took His good enough life and offered it up as a sacrifice on a cross to pay the full price for all of you whose lives are not good enough. And when He was raised from the dead three days later, His new life proved that He will give a new life to all who believe in Him.

"Do you want a new life, Blake Miller?"

"Yeah, I would love a new life, but..."

"When you trust in my Master to be your Savior and your Master, He will start that new life in you right then. He will send the great Helper, the all-powerful Holy Spirit, to live in you, and He will guide and direct you. God's amazing grace in you will give you the desire and the ability to obey God and to do my Master's will.

"So you see, Blake Miller," Tirian continued, "This truly is not about you. It's not about what you can or cannot do. It is all about what my Master can do *for* you and *in* you. All you have to do is to trust Him enough to obey Him and submit your will to His."

"You still don't understand," Miller persisted. "There is some stuff I know your Master doesn't like that I really don't want to give up. I love being in charge of my life and making my own decisions…a lot. I don't think there is any way I could ever give that up."

"I'm sure you can't," Tirian agreed, "but my Master can. And when He lives in a person, it is His power that's at work. He will give you the power to do all the things that you are powerless to do."

"How can that be?"

"After my Master was raised from the dead and returned to His Father in heaven, things went well for my Master's followers for a while, and many joined them in following my Master.

Eventually the enemy got fed up with it and launched a vicious attack against the believers.

"There was one man in particular who Lucifer had a strong influence over. His name was Saul of Tarsus. Saul was well educated and was well respected, especially among the Jewish leaders who hated my Master and His followers. When one of the followers of my Master named Stephen was condemned and killed by the religious leaders, the man Saul was a part of it. He was convinced that the Christians were serving Lucifer."

"Boy, did he have it backwards!" Blake observed.

"Many followers were thrown in prison or killed because of this man. His spies told him that many of the Christians had left Jerusalem and traveled to a distant city, Damascus. When he heard that, Saul got letters of authority from the religious leaders for permission to arrest Christians in Damascus, and he left to go get them. So intent was he to arrest the followers that he traveled through the heat of the day."

"He sounds like a real sweetheart," Blake added.

"On the road to Damascus, suddenly a bright light from heaven illuminated Saul, and my

Master appeared to him. Saul was shocked and fell to the ground. He knew a holy being had come to him, and when he asked Who it was, the words came back, 'I am Jesus Who you are persecuting.'"

"Whoa!" Blake said with surprise. "Did Jesus blast him out of existence for all he had done to His people?"

"No," Tirian answered. "My master told him that He had a special job for him. He was told to go to Damascus to a certain man's house, and someone would come and tell him what Jesus wanted him to do. When the light disappeared, Saul discovered that he was blind. So the men with him led him into the city and to the house my Master had mentioned. For three days Saul didn't eat or drink as he thought about all the evil he had done to Jesus and His followers. Eventually a man was sent by Jesus to heal Saul of his blindness and to teach him. Once Saul became a follower of Jesus, instead of arresting the Christians, he began proclaiming all over the city that Jesus was the Son of God and the Savior of the world. Eventually my Master told this man, who had spent his life hating Jesus, His followers, and anyone who was not a Jew, that he was to go all over the world teaching all of the non-Jews that Jesus was their savior too."

"Go to the people he hated?" Blake asked in amazement. "How could he do that?"

"Saul of Tarsus could not," Tirian announced, "but the new Saul, the follower of Jesus Christ who welcomed my Master into his life, now had the desire and the power to do all that my Master asked him to do.

"It is not about you, Blake Miller, nor was it about Saul of Tarsus: it is all about what my Master can do in anyone who trusts Him."

Chapter Fifteen

Chapter Sixteen

Blake Miller, trembling with fear, huddled in the back of a dark, shallow cave. As he rocked back and forth nervously on the dirty floor, the only things he could think about were what he had heard and experienced since the plane crash. At that moment his future looked very grim, and he had no one to blame but himself.

He looked at the opening of the cave and saw the silhouette of the angel Tirian standing guard in the shadows. He rubbed the sore claw wounds in his arms and his blistered and severely chaffed wrists. Once again he relived the terror of the demons and dangling over the fiery pit. He thought on the angel's words. It was hard to believe that, if he survived this ordeal, there might actually be a chance to avoid an eternity in hell. In his unbelief he had always figured that death wouldn't be so bad. *Boy, was I wrong!* He thought to himself. Once again he fingered the shimmering life line and thought, *Death, when it finally comes for me, is going to be horrible!* Muffled sobs of terror again came from his chest.

Suddenly Tirian hissed a warning. Blake shot a quick look at the angel and saw that he had drawn his sword and was poised to fight. The thought that demons may have found them was overwhelming to the distraught young man. The crippling fear that gripped his soul now threatened to explode into a shriek of terror. Blake knew he must not make any noise that would give away their position, so he slapped both of his hands over his mouth.

Just then he heard it too: a slight rustling sound just outside the cave entrance. He saw Tirian's muscular form lean closer to the opening in preparation for what would happen next.

Suddenly a massive, dark form dropped heavily from above, cutting off all light into the mouth of the cave. Tirian started to lunge forward when they heard the words, "Hold, friend."

"Barcos! You found us!"

"It took some doing," the bronze giant answered. "We had to dodge the demon patrols, plus there are many caves in these rocks, and they're not so easy to spot in this dark realm."

"We?"

"Hey there, Tirian. Did you miss me?" This was said by a small, chubby angel who stepped from behind the bronze giant.

"OH NO!" the silver angel exclaimed. "Barcos, why did you bring him?"

The giant just shrugged his shoulders and looked down at the small newcomer.

"Creedle, you shouldn't be here! It's way too dangerous!"

"But you and Barcos said I could go with you on your next mission!"

"You were supposed to come with us on the mission to get Milton Collins and take him to Paradise," Tirian shot back, "but you weren't there when we were ready to leave."

"Well, I couldn't find my sling," Creedle returned. "You guys wouldn't want me to come to the dark world without my sling, would ya'? I didn't think so! Well, by the time I found it, you'd left without me. You guys had promised to take me with you, an' I couldn't let you go back on your word. So when Barcos came back, I explained it all to him, and here I am!"

"Well, Barcos will just have to take you back," the silver angel announced. "This is no placc for you, Creedle!"

"Too dangerous," Barcos answered. "Too many enemy patrols."

Tirian glared at his huge partner. In response Barcos shrugged again.

"What are you going to do if an army of demons attacks us?" Tirian questioned the small angel with concern.

"I'll use my sling!" Creedle said proudly. "You and Barcos need me, Tirian, 'cause I'm little. I'm so small that I can get into little places. In fact, you two are so huge that the demons will never even notice me. You never know when you might need a little angel."

Tirian understood that, with so many demons looking for them, getting their small friend back to Paradise was out of the question. He also knew from experience that arguing with Creedle was useless. With a deep sigh the silver angel turned back to Barcos. "I'm just glad you made it back to us."

Barcos held up a finger, and the tip began to glow, lighting the cave interior with a dim golden hue. "I see you are still with us, shadowlander," he said with a faint smile.

When Blake was able to see the bronze angel in the light, he noticed several shimmering patches on his arms and shoulder. "You've been wounded," Blake said as he reached up and felt the patched wound on his own left arm.

Barcos snorted indifferently. "Three or four of them were faster than the others, and we had a scuffle. I came off better than they did."

"Were you able to report in?" Tirian asked.

Barcos nodded in the affirmative. "The Master's plan is being implemented now," the bronze giant answered. "We need to start moving the shadowlander back toward the crash."

"Yeah, yeah, that's right!" Creedle repeated enthusiastically. "The Master's got this great plan, an' we need to start movin'!"

"What IS the Master's plan?" Tirian snapped at the smaller angel.

"Oh, I don't know, but it's really amazing!"

"So if you don't know what it is, how do you know it's amazing?" Tirian cross-examined.

"Because it's the Master's," Creedle returned with a knowing smile. "All of the Master's plans are amazing."

Tirian just shook his head. He had known better than to even try.

"We can't leave the cave!" Blake gasped. "The demons can find me out in the open! You know what will happen if they find me! We should stay here!"

"Oh, is this the shadowlander?" the chubby one asked as he marched up to Miller.

"Greetings, favored of the Lord!"

"What are you talking about?" Blake shot back in confusion.

"Oh, that's just something us angels sometimes say to folks," Creedle explained. "I love saying it! I really like the way it sounds."

"I don't care how it sounds," Miller shot back. "I'm not going out there with those demons!"

"Blake Miller," Tirian said firmly, "your only hope is to obey the Master."

"Is He going to save me, Barcos?" Miller asked the bronze giant.

"He has said that, to honor your grandmother, He will help you."

"But will He save me?"

"Only He knows," came the giant's answer.

"But..."

"Our Master has promised to help you, Blake Miller,"Tirian added, "and He has the power to do a lot! We don't know how He will help you, but we know for certain that He will."

With more encouragement the angels got the terrified Miller to stand up and leave the cave. Barcos went first, moving from shadow to shadow, constantly alert for any sound that betrayed the presence of the demons.

"I can't believe I'm on a real mission with you guys!" Creedle whispered excitedly from behind. "This is so awesome!"

Immediately they stopped, and all of the others turned and stared at the plump little angel. "What?" he asked looking from one to the other.

"Little buddy," Barcos asked patiently, "can you be quiet?"

"Who, me? Well…yeah, I can be quiet. I can be real quiet. I can be so quiet that nobody will even know I'm here. You guys won't believe how quiet I can…"

"Creedle!" Tirian hissed.

"Hmm?"

"There are demons all around us," the silver angel explained. "We need you to be quiet…now."

"You mean right now?"

"Yes, right now."

"Oh," the small angel answered with an understanding nod. His eyes grew very wide, and he put his finger on his lips.

Barcos then turned and continued leading them down the rocky hill.

They moved slowly so as not to make any sound as they traveled except for the faint crunch of the cinders under their feet. On reaching a large boulder not too far from the place where the plane crash was visible, Barcos led them into the deep shadow next to it.

"Wait, wait, wait!" Blake hissed in a panic. "I hear them! We've got to go back!"

He started to rush back the way they had come, but Creedle, who was standing behind him, began to push against him and said, "Just hold on there, buster!"

Tirian also grabbed his hand and held him firmly in place.

"No!" Blake said as he struggled to free himself. "We've got to get away from here!"

"Blake Miller," Tirian said firmly but in a low voice. "Do you want to escape hell?"

"What? Of course I do!"

"If you go back to the cave, there is no hope for you," Tirian said again, still gripping Blake's hand. "Our Master has promised to help you. You need to believe that He will and do your part."

"My part! What's my part—except getting burned up forever?"

"Yes, Blake Miller," Tirian shot back angrily, "getting burned up forever is your part—if you reject my Master again and follow your own will like you've done in the past.

"One thing I know for sure, and that is, without my Master, there is no hope for you…none! So make your choice right now before Barcos, Creedle, and I risk anymore for you. Will you trust in my Master, or are you going to do what you've always done and trust in yourself?"

Hearing the evil voices of the demons nearby was terrifying to Blake, but the pain from their claws piercing his arms and the burns from the flames of the pit were still fresh. Finally he looked at Tirian and said, "What does your Master want me to do?"

The silver angel turned and nodded to Barcos.

"Alright, follow me," Barcos ordered. "We must move closer."

"Okay, okay,I will go with you if that's what your Master wants," Miller returned anxiously, "but I don't understand why we have to get closer to the demons? We should be staying as far from the demons as we can."

"When our Master provides your help," Barcos whispered, "you will need to return to your body. The further you are away from your injured self, the easier it is for the enemies to capture you, and you know what to expect if that happens.

"Alright," Barcos spoke again, "follow me, stay in the shadows, and don't make a sound."

As he said this, both he and Tirian turned and looked hard at the smaller angel.

Seeing their eyes locked on him, Creedle covered his mouth with his hand and nodded his head.

With the bronze giant leading, the four crept from shadow to shadow, inching ever closer to the scene of the crash.

"Find that scum's life line," Blake heard the boss demon call out.

In response to this order, three demons rushed to the thick brush where the airplane seat that contained Blake's injured body still lay, each one eager to comply with their leader's demand.

"Here it is, boss!" one of the demons called out and snatched up the flickering cord. Immediately the minion screamed, grabbed his hand, and dropped the lifeline.

"You boulder head!" the boss yelled at the injured lackey. "You can't let it touch your skin! Use your sword to lift it up and trace it that way!"

"Oh, right...right," the injured demon said and pulled out his sword to lift the cord.

The boss rolled his yellow eyes and snarled, "Why are all the dumb ones assigned to me?"

"I got it, boss!" the demon called. "See, I got it with my sword, just like you said!"

"WELL, FOLLOW IT!" the boss screamed. "AND YOU TWO GO WITH HIM! IF YOU FIND THAT GUY, BRING HIM TO ME ON THE DOUBLE! YOU GOT THAT?"

"Uh…yeah, boss, we got it," the demon with the cord returned. "But…uh…once we get 'im, where are you gonna be…you know, so's we can bring 'im to you."

"The rest of the company and I will be right here," the boss returned, "just in case those angels try to sneak him back to his body. NOW FIND HIM!"

Chapter Sixteen

Chapter Seventeen

"Sir Milton, Child of the King!"

Milton was just exiting a beautiful mansion where he had been visiting with one of his new friends. He looked for the source of the call and saw an angelic messenger in a glowing robe standing in the golden street.

"Are you Drialla?" Milton asked. "I got a message on my white stone that I needed to meet the angel Drialla."

"At your service," the angel said with a slight nod. "The Master has reserved a place for you in the next session of Life Class, and it is ready to begin. If you will please join the others behind me, I will take all of you there to begin your class."

"Certainly," Milton said with a smile.

"Until next time, my good friend!" Milton said to his companion who stood on the steps of the mansion and waved. He then joined the three others behind Drialla.

The angel faced the four and addressed Milton, "Sir Milton, it is my honor to introduce you to Lady Abeja, Sir Robert, and Sir Nazir.

"To the rest of you, I am delighted to introduce Sir Milton."

"I can't tell you how glad I am to meet each of you!" Milton said genuinely.

"It's like everyone here is your family, isn't it?" Nazir returned warmly with an understanding smile.

"Yes," Milton said with a laugh, "it is!"

"And everything is so beautiful!" Abeja said as she looked around.

"Favored of the Lord," Drialla said, addressing them all, "our Master wants everyone who comes here to learn how to fully enjoy and utilize all of the beauty and wonders of Paradise. That is why He created the Life Class. Your class is about to begin, so if you will all please follow me, I will take you there now."

As Drialla stepped forward, the four behind her followed. Suddenly Milton realized that they were passing rapidly along the street. As he looked down, it appeared to Milton that his feet weren't actually touching the golden street.

"Wow!" he thought to himself, "Jesus was right! I love these shoes!"

They traveled a long way, but it took almost no time for them to get there. Drialla stopped in front of a mountain with a massive waterfall hundreds of feet high. "This stunning waterfall is one of the Master's gifts to those who come here!" the angel announced proudly. "Your Life Class will be held in the grotto located behind the falls. Come this way."

Following a wide walkway made of coral bricks and lined on both sides with shrubs containing the most beautiful and fragrant purple flowers, the angel led them into a gigantic, cave-like opening behind the cascading water. Milton was stunned! There had to be several thousand people sitting in ornately carved, throne-like chairs all around the outside edge of the grotto.

Drialla led them up to four empty thrones and informed them that these were their seats. "Your class will start momentarily," the angel said.

"Will we need to take notes?" Milton asked with concern.

Drialla smiled and said, "Here you will remember it all." Still smiling, the angel suddenly disappeared.

As Milton visited with his new friends, they became aware of soft, sweet music filling the large cavern. Though the massive waterfall was nearby, none of its roaring noise entered the grotto. Looking around for the source of the music, Milton saw gigantic, bright, colorful images forming in the large, open center of the large cave. Flowing and swirling in and around rapidly changing pictures was a radiant, living, bluish-grey essence that Milton knew to be the Spirit of God. The images were formed by what appeared to be hundreds of thousands of tiny pinpoints of light, each able to change in brightness and color.

The lights formed into the image of an ocean with large, crashing waves, then suddenly changed into a gigantic whale that swam around the grotto. Dolphins appeared and danced with the whale. Other sea creatures appeared that Milton had never seen before and joined in the celebration. The music became louder and more powerful and moving. Just then all the lights began to whirl like a kaleidoscope of shapes and colors. When the music reached its magnificent end, all of the lights stopped and formed a large golden halo in the center of the room.

"I greet all of you in the name of our wonderful and loving King!" said a man who stepped into the lighted center of the golden halo. "My name is Enoch. I am humbled to have been asked by the Master to be your teacher for the Life Class, but Jesus said that it is fitting, because very few have been here longer than I have.

"All of you who have recently arrived from the land of shadows are familiar with the saying that a picture is worth a thousand words.'" At this point the halo surrounding Enoch morphed into a magnificent, snowcapped mountain range, filling almost the entire grotto. "But in our case," Enoch continued, raising his arms to call attention to the beautiful vision of the mountains, "an image created by the Spirit of God is worth all the words a man could ever speak!"

Milton's mouth dropped open as he viewed the stunning vision before all of them. The detail was amazing! He could even see clouds drifting over the peaks and an avalanche of snow tumbling down a jagged draw.

"All of you know well the laws of nature and the principles of life required to exist in the land of shadows where we all once lived," Enoch said. "But those were the laws and principles of a fallen world. While there is much here in Paradise that is similar to the world you once knew, it is clearly not the same. This world is not fallen!

There is no influence of sin, evil, or the failures of people for that matter. Almost everything in this wonderful place has been made by God and is exactly the way He intends it to be. In point of fact, the only thing here made by man are the wounds in the hands, feet, and side of Jesus Christ, our Savior and King."

A somber feeling came over all of them as they realized that their past sins were the reason for those wounds.

"Because Paradise is a pure and unblemished place, the laws of eternal life and the principles of living in joy are different here than what you knew in the shadow world. Instructing you in these wonderful truths is what this class is all about. We will talk about all of the amazing things God has created here for you to enjoy. We will also talk about what the Master wants you to know in order for you to appreciate His gifts to the absolute fullest. And let me say from the outset, that all of the wonderful things you will learn, as well as all of God's astounding gifts to us, will each reveal more and more to you about the awe-inspiring God we worship. And that, my friends, is what eternal life is all about. Take it from one who has enjoyed the magnificence of this place much longer than almost any other here…You will be absolutely and immeasurably thrilled at what the Most High God, His Glorious Son, and their indescribably wonderful Holy Spirit show you! And everything you learn here will move you to love and worship our God more!"

Chapter Seventeen

Chapter Eighteen

The little beagle looked terrible. He was extremely thin and had a dull hair coat, tattered ears, and scabs covered his legs and face. He obviously hadn't been cared for in quite some time.

The year before, a hunter had brought a truck load of fifteen hunting dogs into the woods and turned them loose to track rabbits. He and his friends bought, sold, and traded dogs all the time, so he was not particularly attached to any of them. As long as they ran rabbits, he was satisfied.

The number of dogs he owned varied from time to time. There had been occasions when he owned as many as thirty dogs. With so many animals he decided that, for convenience's sake, he would name them all, male or female, "Lady." When he needed to call his dogs, he didn't want to have to think of thirty different names. The savvy hunter wanted to be able to holler, "COME HERE, LADY," and have thirty dogs come charging at him.

During a hunt the previous fall, after the pack had sniffed out the trail of a rabbit and raced in pursuit, the smallest male found himself, as usual, in the back of the pack. With his short legs and the rough terrain, he continued to lose ground throughout the hunt.

The leaders of the pack could tell that the scent of the rabbit they trailed was fresh, which fanned their hunting instincts into a consuming passion. The other dogs sprinted instinctively after the others Being so powerfully motivated, they raced in pursuit of the escaping hare, bawling for all they were worth.

The hounds were so focused on the prey they were tracking that the lot of them sprinted right past another rabbit hiding close by. After the howling pack of dogs had rushed past, the hidden bunny decided to hurry to a safer location and quickly darted off.

When it burst from its place of concealment, it ran right in front of the little male dog that was trailing behind. The rabbit's sudden appearance so startled the small hound that it stopped in its tracks and immediately bawled an alarm to the others that he had found their prey. Confidently he raced after this new victim.

With all the racket the pack was making, the sound of the little beagle's howl soon faded as he ran the opposite direction. When night came, the solitary dog discovered that he had lost both the rabbit and his pack.

The beagle wandered for a while, trying to pick up either the sound or the scent of the other hounds, but he detected nothing. Being the smallest and used to fending for himself, the young dog took stock of his surroundings. He found a puddle of dirty water to quench his thirst. Later he had a supper of grubs and earthworms dug out from under a rotted log. When the sun went down, the exhausted dog curled up in a pile of leaves and slept.

Life was hard for the lost hound for the next year, but he managed to survive in the woods by eating lizards, snakes, insects, and an occasional rabbit.

That morning the quietness of the forest had been broken by the explosion of the plane crash. Though it happened over a mile away from the hollow log where the beagle had been asleep, the distant noise startled the dog as well as every other animal in the area. Most of the forest creatures fled the terrible noise, but a strange, compelling curiosity gripped the little hound, and he began trotting toward the source of the sound.

Some of the fallen trees he encountered were so rotten that it only took a little effort to claw his way over them. Others were large enough that he was forced to find a way around them. But on he went, something strong deep inside pushing him to keep going.

The beagle came to a wide creek, the swift waters of which made him balk. At this point the little dog actually started to give up the strange quest, but again the call deep within compelled him to search for a way.

As he trotted along the bank, he eventually spotted a dead tree that had fallen across the swift, flowing water. Jumping up on the narrow bridge, he made the scary crossing, leaping happily off the log on the other side and continuing on his mission.

Soon he smelled the acrid smoke of burning fuel and debris. As he arrived in the area of the scene of the crash, the smoke and fumes seared the inside of his sensitive nose, but still he pressed on. The closer he got to the destroyed plane, the more urgent seemed the call.

As the small beagle crept cautiously into the charred clearing where the burning remnants of the destroyed plane lay, a faint, familiar scent reached his nose. There were so many competing smells that he only got an occasional whiff. He paused for a moment, turning in circles, sniffing the polluted air.

It took him a moment to separate the unique odor from the fumes, the smoke, and the soot, but finally he got it. He knew this scent, and it brought to him distant, pleasant memories. Slowly, and being careful not to lose it in the cacophony of strange smells, he tracked the familiar aroma. It led him away from the burning, twisted body of the crashed plane. It seemed to be coming from a think clump of weeds and brush just beyond the charred clearing.

The closer he came to the source of the captivating smell, the more urgency the little beagle felt. As he stepped quickly into the brush, the first thing he saw was the jagged metal of the airplane seat that had been ripped from its attachment to the plane's floor. Circling the seat, he stopped short, staring at what was before him. Now he remembered why the smell was so familiar. A human was lying on his side, strapped in the seat. The figure before him seemed to be completely unresponsive, but urgency still pressed him.

Extending his sensitive nose toward the figure, he sniffed. He smelled blood, lots of blood, but there was something else. He moved closer until the end of his snout touched the human's. What was it he smelled? It was faint, but it was there. It was…it was…LIFE!

The demons had watched the whole scenario play out. When they saw the emaciated beagle and all of the blood flowing down Blake's face, the boss got excited. "*He, he, he*! Watch this, you roaches! That starving cur's smelled blood. He'll finish this guy off quick for us!"

But instead of attacking the injured man, the pitiful little hound licked the injured face and began bellowing an incredibly loud howl.

"NO!" shouted the demon boss. "THAT FILTHY BEAST WILL ATTRACT SOMEONE'S ATTENTION WITH ALL THAT YEOWLING! STOP HIM!"

Immediately several of the demons moved closer and began fanning their large wings powerfully.

The blast of wind caught the small dog off guard, and he was knocked off his feet and rolled backwards against a large pine tree close by, painfully bruising his ribs.

Both Tirian and Barcos sensed that something significant was happening. Grabbing Blake and signaling for Creedle to follow, they hurried as fast as they dared closer to the crash.

When they got near enough to view the scene, they spotted the demons trying to drive the dog away from Blake's injured form. At first Miller thought that the demons were entertaining themselves by tormenting the poor little dog, but as he watched, he saw something amazing happen.

With difficulty the beagle managed to right itself in the turbulent wind from the demon's wings and, digging his claws into the earth, dragged himself back to Blake's side. His short little legs braced widely apart, the beagle once again began sending out an ear-shattering howl that could be clearly heard over a mile away.

"He's calling for help!" Tirian whispered encouragingly in Blake's ear from behind one of the large boulders where they watched the drama play out.

"HE WON'T STOP, BOSS!" one of the flapping demons yelled.

With a fierce snarl the leader of the fallen angels stomped forward. He angrily knocked his underlings out of the way and, extending a gnarly claw toward the brave little dog, the boss bellowed, "COME!"

"What's he doing?" Blake hissed as he watched from the shadows.

"Nothing good," Tirian answered.

"He is calling for help from the land of shadows," Barcos added.

"Who in the land of shadows helps demons?" Creedle asked in a low voice.

As they watched, to Blake's horror, a large copperhead snake suddenly slithered out from some leaves. The poisonous snake lifted its head and seemed to look at the demon's extended claw before it turned and went straight for the beagle.

Chapter Nineteen

When the short, pudgy angel saw the large copperhead snake headed toward the brave beagle, he jerked out his sling and announced with determination, "Not on my watch!"

Quickly Tirian grabbed Creedle and pulled him behind the boulder. "You can't!" he whispered in his small friend's ear.

"We've got to stop that snake!" the chubby angel demanded.

"We can't show ourselves, little one," Barcos said in a low voice. "We only have one chance to save the shadowlander. If the demons find us now, all is lost."

"But…"

"I hate it too, Creedle," Tirian consoled, "but Blake Miller is our first concern."

So intent was the small beagle on his howling that he didn't see the snake until it was right in front of him. The hound spotted the quick movement as the fangs shot for his neck. With reflexes honed from surviving in the dangerous woods, the beagle threw himself backwards just out of reach of the deadly venom.

Now the little dog's attention was on the immediate threat, and he curled his lips back in a fierce snarl.

The copperhead was not intimidated and slithered forward, intent on its demonic mission. Rushing again to confront its adversary, the snake coiled quickly and struck.

Again the hound was ready and sprang to the side as the deadly, open jaws whiffed past. In an instant the beagle leaped on the serpent, grabbing it in the middle of its long body, shaking it violently.

Now the snake was in trouble, and it desperately snapped the air, trying to sink its fangs into any part of its attacker.

Suddenly the beagle released the snake's body and screamed in intense pain. Looking for the source of the agony, he spotted the serpent latched onto his right foreleg. Furious, the hound snapped hard, grabbing the snake right behind its head. The hound locked his powerful jaws on the serpent's neck and bit fiercely. At the same time he jerked the snake free from his leg and viciously shook the hated creature until its head popped off.

Casting the dead serpent aside, the injured beagle hobbled painfully back in front of the injured human. Once again he licked Miller's face and howled with even more intensity.

"Hey, Dickson, do you hear that?" Deputy Randall Phelps asked as they stood beside their patrol cars on a blacktop road between the towns of Loachapoka and Notasulga, Alabama, west of Auburn.

"Yeah, it's just some dog howlin'."

"But it's comin' from down there at the crash site," Phelps persisted. "What if it's one of 'em's pet that survived?"

"Nothin' survived that plane crash," Dickson returned flatly. "It's just some stray huntin' dog. You can tell cause he ain't barkin'. He's howlin'."

Just then more locals in pickup trucks came cruising slowly by, trying to see the crash.

"Hey, Deputy," the man on the passenger side said as they pulled up. "Is that where it crashed? Me an' Jerry saw it come down."

"Yeah, it hit in the woods behind us," Dickson answered.

"Everybody dead?"

"We can't give out that information yet…but it was pretty bad, if you know what I mean."

"Well, listen, Deputy," the man continued, "I've got a cousin, Wilfred Lawson…maybe you know him. Well, ol' Wilfred, he always makes a big donation to the Sheriff's Fund Drive ever' year, so as sort of a favor to Wilfred, me an' Jerry was wonderin' if we could go in there an' see if we could get us a piece of a perpeller or somethin' from that plane. You never know. It might be worth a few bucks one of these days."

"Listen, fellas," Phelps said, stepping up. "We got emergency vehicles coming, and we need to keep this road open, so you need to move along."

"Right," agreed Dickson, taking his cue from Phelps. "Emergency crews are comin' so keep moving."

After the left, Phelps looked back toward the path through the woods that the EMTs made when they removed the bodies. "Somethings not right, Dickson. That dog's still howling."

"So?" Dickson answered. "Just let him howl. What does it matter?"

"Do you think he might be hung up on some of the wreckage?"

"Who cares? It's just a stray. Hey, look! There are the lights of the fire trucks finally getting here!"

Just then they heard the howl turn into an intense cry of pain. "That dog's hurt!" exclaimed Phelps and dashed back into the woods.

"Boss!" one of the demons exclaimed when he saw Phelps rushing through the woods. "It's one of the shadowlanders!"

"That miserable cur is calling them!" the boss snarled. "Stop that man! Drive him back into the woods!"

All of the demons began flapping their wings, producing a gale of wind in the face of the deputy. Phelps threw his arms up to protect his eyes from the dirt, sticks, and sand that suddenly blasted into his face. Strangely, the powerful rush of wind suddenly stopped, and Phelps continued hurrying toward the crying dog.

"WHAT?" the demon boss yelled in the midst of their flapping. "Where did that little shrimp come from?"

Hovering in front of Deputy Phelps was Creedle. He was blocking the savage wind produced by the demons with his small, extended wings.

Tirain and Barcos realized what the small angel was doing the same time the demons did. "Come on!" the bronze giant yelled. "They'll cut him to ribbons!" Suddenly blinding light burst from the bodies of the two angel warriors as they roared the name of their Master and charged at the demons.

As Phelps ran up, he could see that the dog's right front leg, shoulder, and neck were swollen to three times their normal size, and the dog was having a hard time barking. When Phelps arrived, the hound turned and threw himself on Blake.

The deputy quickly knelt beside Miller and put two fingers on his carotid artery. Grabbing the microphone of his service radio, he pushed the button and cried, "WE GOT ANOTHER CRASH VICTIM DOWN HERE, AN' HE'S ALIVE!"

"Alive?" the voice on the radio shot back.

"YES! HE'S ALIVE! GET THE EMT'S DOWN HERE QUICK! AND GET THAT AMBULENCE BACK!"

Tirian and Barcos had charged straight into the group of demons, taking out two of them instantly. The shock of the unexpected attack by the angels had surprised the demons and driven them back. The boss quickly saw that it was only two and rallied his warriors to fight.

Tirian suddenly found himself furiously engaged with three demons while Barcos was surrounded by five. A black sword creased Tirian's upper arm, and grey, steamy smoke began to trail from the wound. In the midst of his furious flailing and chopping, Barcos suddenly received a slice across his neck and another to his arm.

"CHOP THEM TO PIECES!" the boss demon screamed to his fighters.

Just then a bright ball of light flew past the two fighting angels and struck the boss between his eyes. With a terrible scream of pain, the demon leader grabbed his face and fell back. Instantly another radiant sphere zipped into the shoulder of one the warriors attacking the bronze giant. Screaming in agony, he too fled the battle field. When a third bright missile painfully creased the head of another, the rest of the demons had enough. With anxious cries, the furious enemy fighters retreated.

Barcos and Tirian looked back and saw Creedle hovering above the wreckage just behind them, grimly staring at the retreating enemy fighters. He held his sling in his hand, loaded with another of his light balls, and had his fist on his hip like a super hero.

"Good job, little one!" Barcos called as he sheathed his sword and began patching their wounds.

"See, Tirian," the small, pudgy angel said with a confident smile, "you guys need me!"

Chapter Twenty

By the time the fire trucks arrived, the crews already knew of the crash survivor. They grabbed their medical equipment and pushed hurriedly through the woods. Deputy Phelps saw them coming and waved them to his location.

After checking Miller's vital signs, one of the crew pulled out a portable radio and began explaining to the on-call medical staff at the nearest hospital what he was seeing. As soon as the hospital staff understood that the firefighter was trained in emergency medicine, they had him start an IV line on Miller and give fluids to counteract shock and blood loss.

After answering more questions about Miller's condition, the hospital staff determined that the firefighters could move him away from the crash scene. Unbuckling the seat belt, the firemen very gently lifted the injured man and placed him on a blanket that had been spread nearby. Realizing that Blake had multiple cuts and lacerations as well as a head injury, there was concern that he might have some internal injuries that could not be evaluated at that moment. It appeared to the emergency people tending him that the metal seat had protected him when he was thrown from the plane.

Until the ambulance arrived, the only other thing the firefighters could do was to bandage his multiple wounds. A blanket was then spread over the injured man, and six of the firemen grabbed the edge of the blanket he was on and carried him up through the woods to the road.

"Go with them, Blake Miller," Tirian called. "Stay close to your injured self!"

Just then they heard more screams, and more demonic reinforcements landed in front of them.

"HURRY, BLAKE MILLER!" Tirian yelled when he saw the squad of enemy fighters preparing to attack. "GO!"

"I…I can't!" Miller called back from the edge of the boulder. The appearance of more of the warriors had paralyzed him with fear. "There's no place to hide out there! The demons will catch me in the open!"

"CREEDLE!" the silver angel cried. "GO WITH HIM! YOU MUST KEEP HIM WITH HIS INJURED SELF!"

"Yes, sir!" the small angel returned and flew quickly behind Miller. "Okay, buster," he announced, "we got to go!" With those words Creedle shoved Miller forward.

Terrified, Blake tried to grab the rock to keep from being pushed out into the open. When the short, pudgy angel saw that he was resisting, Creedle furiously flapped his wings and literally drove the reluctant Miller in pursuit of the firefighters.

"I'LL BE BACK!" the faithful little angel called over his shoulder as he and the terrified human entered the woods.

"NO!" he heard Tirian call after him. "STAY WITH BLAKE MILLER!" As he said these words, the two large angelic warriors positioned themselves between the demons and the medical people tending the injured crash victim.

By the time the struggling firemen managed to get Miller through the thick woods and up onto the road, the ambulance was arriving. Jumping out, the Emergency Medical staff quickly assessed the injured man. Drugs to prevent shock were quickly administered through the IV line, and with the help of the firemen, Blake was loaded into the back of the ambulance.

"Come on!" Creedle ordered as he pushed Miller ahead. "You need to stay with yourself! *Hee, hee, hee…*.'stay with yourself.' That sounds so dumb."

As Blake started to step into the emergency vehicle, the door slammed in his face. "Keep going!" the little angel snapped and pushed both of them through the closed door like it was made out of air.

Once inside, Blake looked around and realized that there was a slight transparency to everything. One of the EMTs walked over and reached through Blake to grab a stethoscope.

"Whoa!" Miller said with a shiver as the man's arm passed through his body. "This is going to take some getting used to."

One of the demon leaders screamed a war cry, and twenty warriors charged the two angels resolutely standing between them and their victim. With cries of "FOR THE KING OF GLORY!" Tirian and Barcos, light radiating from their bodies, charged into the furious mass of enemy warriors with powerful sweeps of their swords. The power of their attack stopped the charging demons. The two angels swung their weapons so swiftly that their swords were a blur. When the enemy warriors tried to surround them, Tirian and Barcos quickly turned back to back and continued to rain powerful and rapid blows upon the swords of their attackers.

Just then the demon leader blew a loud note on a trumpet he carried around his neck. In response, a large horde of demons came flying over the hill.

When the two angels saw the number of fighters in the new group, they knew they were in trouble. But instead of calling the small army of demons to help them destroy the two angels, the demon leader screamed and pointed to the departing ambulance.

"THEY'RE GOING AFTER BLAKE MILLER AND CREEDLE!" Tirian cried in a panic.

"WE MUST GO TO THEM NOW!" Barcos roared. At the same instant both of the large angels launched straight into the air and shot after the ambulance like two rockets.

The demons were stunned at the rapid retreat of the two angels, and in confusion turned to face their leader.

"HURRY!" the demon chief roared, "GATHER OUR WARRIORS, AND WE WILL

CRUSH THEM ALL! I WILL HAVE THAT SHADOWLANDER!"

With a chorus of war cries, the demons hurled themselves into the air and rushed to join the large, wicked band positioning themselves to attack those in the ambulance.

"Are you okay?" Creedle asked his companion. "You don't look so good."

"I don't know what's happening!" Blake grunted as he bent over in obvious pain and began staggering uncontrollably toward his injured self. Just then the injured Blake Miller began groaning and stirring on the gurney.

"He's coming to!" one of EMTs called to his partner riding in the back of the ambulance and rushed to attend to the injured man.

With a scream Blake was suddenly sucked inside his battered body, and at the same instant the injured man on the gurney yelled and began flailing his arms.

"Hold him down!"

"HELP ME!" Miller roared. "IT HURTS!"

One of the EMTs threw himself across Blake in an effort to restrain his thrashing "I'll try to hold him down!" he yelled at his companion. "Quick, give him a sedative"

"I'm pulling it up now!" the other shouted back.

Tossing the empty drug vial aside, he rushed over and injected the medication straight into Blake's IV line. As the drug took effect, the injured man's violent tossing grew less and less.

Creedle's attention was suddenly drawn to what was happening in the spiritual realm above the racing ambulance. Shooting through the top of the vehicle, he stood defiantly on the roof, staring at the gathering crowd of angry demons preparing for their attack.

Seeing the overwhelming odds before him, the courageous little angel whipped out his sling and loaded it with one of the shining spheres.

"Creedle!" a weak voice called from below. Looking down through the roof of the ambulance, the small warrior saw the spirit of Blake Miller pushing up from his unconscious body. "What's happening?"

"Those black-hearted snakes are coming after you!" Creedle answered. "Their boss is screaming that he will have you. But don't you worry! They'll have to get through ME to get you!"

Just then, far above them, Blake heard the demon leader yell and saw the brigade of fiendish warriors dropping like a wicked waterfall to claim their victim.

Bright light began to radiate from the small angel as he stood firm, resolving to give his all to defend his charge. He had just started to whirl his sling when instantly Tirian and Barcos, glowing brightly, were beside him.

Seeing the great, fighting angels of God suddenly appear with their radiant swords drawn to oppose them, the leader of the evil horde halted the charge. The demon boss pulled out his horn and began blowing for reinforcements.

"I know this guy is not a follower of the Master, but can we get some help?" Creedle asked with concern when he saw the army of wicked warriors hovering over them. "Even a few angels would be helpful."

"Help would already be here if they were coming," Tirian snapped back.

"The King must have the host battling somewhere else," Barcos surmised.

"I'm afraid it's up to us," Tirian added.

"Well, we're going to need help from somewhere!" Creedle exclaimed.

"What about his Nana?" Barcos asked.

"Yes!" cried Tirian. "Creedle, we need you to go to his grandmother, Lady Edith."

"Lady Edith is this guy's grandmother?" Creedle said in disbelief. "She's awesome! With a grandmother like her, how come he doesn't follow the Master?"

"It's his choice," Tirian answered. "But Lady Edith's prayers are the reason we are here fighting for him. So go to her and get her praying for her grandson Blake Miller."

"How do I get to her?"

The silver angel reached into a pocket and drew out a rounded, oval, glowing disc. He covered it with his hand, and when he uncovered it, there was an image of Edith Miller radiating from it.

"Take this," Tirian said, handing the luminescent object to the small angel. "Command it to take you to Lady Edith, and it will."

"This is so fun!" Creedle said with a laugh. "I've always wanted to use one of these!"

"Just hurry!"

"Right!" the small angel said, holding up the glowing disc. "TO LADY EDITH!"

Chapter Twenty

Chapter Twenty-One

Abeja, Nazir, Robert, and Milton were sitting on some of the large boulders decorating the shore of the lake below the massive falls. Sir Enoch's class had ended, but they were so mesmerized by what they had learned that they wanted to sit in this beautiful place together and discuss it.

"Sir Enoch said that the Spirit of God is everywhere," Nazir said. "That means we can't get away from Him."

"Who would want to?" Abeja returned. "All I ever feel is loved. It's wonderful!"

"Can you sense His presence around these rocks we are sitting on?" Milton asked as he rested his hands on the cool stone surface. As he did so, the visible presence of the Holy Spirit wafted across the surface of the rocks and floated around and into his hands.

"Wait! Do you hear something?" said Robert, who was doing the same thing. "There's a deep resonance coming from the rocks. I can feel it in my soul."

"Yes, I can hear it!" Milton added excitedly. "Listen to it! It's a song about the greatness of God! *'The Lord is our sure foundation, our stronghold; He has taken us out of a place of fear and put our feet on a firm, solid rock that cannot be shaken.'*"

"Isn't that amazing?" Nazir asked as he also rested his hands on the boulder. "Even the rocks sing praise here."

"It's so much more than I can comprehend...even in this perfect place!" Abeja exclaimed. "Whenever I seek the presence of the Holy Spirit within me, a sense of love, joy, and acceptance so overwhelms me that I almost can't stand it! His love...His joy...it's too much! I feel like I'm going to burst from the beauty and wonder of it."

"I've felt that too," Milton admitted.

Just then all of them were alerted by a message on the white stone in their rings.

"The King is calling me," Milton said.

"Me too," agreed Abeja.

"Mine says I'm called to a banquet with Jesus," Robert put in.

"It looks like all of us are going," Nazir said with a smile as he read his own message.

Within moments another angel appeared and led them to the King's banquet hall. As was every other structure in Paradise, this room was massive. The lofty ceiling far above was held up by many ornately carved, giant pillars, some of jade, some of onyx, some of coral, and some of red jasper. Thousands of large, circular, ivory tables filled the vast chamber. The tables were surrounded by ten ivory, throne-like chairs, each with plush cushions.

The angel led the four friends to one of the tables and showed them their places as many thousands of others were also led to their seats. Beautiful music wafted through the air while Milton and his friends introduced themselves to the five others at their table. It was during the introductions and greetings that Milton noticed that there was an empty chair beside him. Looking around the vast chamber, he noticed that a chair was empty at every table that he could see.

"Greetings to all of you, my bride!" an excited voice boomed over the entire room. Looking up, Milton saw the Son of God hovering in the air over the middle of the room. He was grinning with delight at all of His guests. "I cannot tell you how much I have longed to eat this meal with you!"

Jesus began to describe the love the Father felt for each of them and that His life on earth and His death on the cross visualized that great love for them. As He spoke, the Holy Spirit filled them, expressing in a nonverbal way God's immeasurable and powerful love to their hearts. Milton was overwhelmed at the intensity that was directed at him at that moment.

Eventually Jesus told them that He wanted to share His Supper with them anew, and instantly there were loaves of unleavened bread in His hands. Thanking the Father, Jesus tossed the loaves upward, and they exploded into thousands of pieces that flew through the air to the guests. Suddenly a broken piece appeared before Milton, and he took it.

Jesus held up His own piece and asked, "What is this bread that you hold?"

All of those in the room lifted their pieces toward their Savior and cried, "IT IS YOUR BODY!"

"It is for you!" Jesus called back. "It is all for you, beloved of God! Now each of you have experienced that everything I am and all that I have is yours. Join Me as we eat it together!" After saying this, the resurrected Lord ate His piece, and all the others worshipfully did the same.

Suddenly a golden challis and a golden pitcher were in Christ's hands. As he began pouring wine from the pitcher into His cup, He said, "This wine is My blood that has covered you all and has redeemed you. It is the blood of the covenant that the Father, the Spirit, and I have made with each of you."

As the King made this announcement, wine appeared out of the air in front of Milton and the others and filled the golden cups in front of each of them. After thanking the Father for the wine, Jesus raised His cup and cried out, "What is this wine?"

"IT IS YOUR BLOOD!" the guests called out as they lifted their cups.

"It was poured out in love for each of you!" the Master cried. "Be assured that greater love has no man than this—that He lay down His life for His friends. Join Me, My dear friends!" the King called and lifted the cup to His mouth.

As Milton drank from his, he was stunned at how delicious it tasted.

Just then there was a swirl of glowing, bluish vapors in the empty chair, and suddenly the vapors took the form of a person sitting with them. As Milton stared at the revealed presence of the Spirit of God, the face of Jesus smiling at them appeared on the Spirit's form.

"Sweet Spirit," Abeja exclaimed, "I didn't realize that you looked like our Lord!"

"You'll notice, dear Abeja," the Holy Spirit answered, still smiling, "that I can sound like Him too. You shouldn't be surprised. Jesus and I are one, as We are with the Father. Surely you know by now that I can take any form and sound in any way that the Father and the Son desire. I have no limitations. As I am hosting your table now, so I am hosting at each of the tables, and so I am also right now with each of the followers of the Father still living in the shadow world.

"For each of you," the Spirit continued, "the Father has prepared this banquet to welcome you home." As He said this, the Spirit lifted His arms, and large golden platters appeared in front of each of them, heaped high with the most amazing food Milton had ever seen.

"Eat, my dear beloved friends!" the Spirit of God called with a beautiful smile. "Eat and enjoy the wonderful delights your loving Father has prepared especially for you! Taste and see that the Lord is good!"

Chapter Twenty-Two

Edith Miller was a woman of strong habits. She had eaten her afternoon snack of a bagel topped with cream cheese and raspberry jelly. Now she was busily engaged in taking her usual nap.

Creedle arrived in her bedroom almost instantly after leaving his friends. The first thing he spotted was a photograph of Blake Miller in a beautiful silver frame on the stand beside her bed.

"Yep," the little angel said out loud as he looked at the photo, "I'm definitely in the right place."

A noise close by alerted him and he noticed the older woman snoozing in the bed. Seeing Lady Edith sleeping soundly caused the little angel some concern.

"Prayer warrior or not, she won't be doing much praying while she's asleep.

"Lady Edith," Creedle said gently as he leaned down near the woman's ear. He got no response.

"Come on now, Lady Edith!" he said much louder. "You got to wake up an' start praying!"

Other than the droning buzz coming from the older woman's nose, there was again no response.

"LADY EDITH!" Creedle screamed in her face. "YOUR GRANDSON NEEDS YOU RIGHT NOW! YOU KNOW WHO I'M TALKING ABOUT? YOUR GRANDSON…BLAKE MILLER? HE NEEDS YOU TO PRAY FOR HIM! NOW! RIGHT NOW!"

Again there was no reaction.

Starting to panic, the little angel reached down to grab the sleeping woman and shake her, but his hands passed straight through her. With a look of horror on his face, Creedle watched the old saint snooze on, absorbed by her dream.

"'Great Master, Tirian and Barcos are in trouble, and I can't wake her up! What can I do? She can't see me, hear me, or feel me! I'm trying my best to wake her up, but she's busy dreaming!' WAIT…SHE'S DREAMING! Maybe I can enter her dream. Some of the angels do that on occasion. Surely it can't be that hard."

Creedle quickly flew to her side and placed his hands on her head. Closing his eyes, the little angel concentrated very hard and began to speak. As he did so, his hands began to glow.

"Lady Edith."

The soundly sleeping woman slowly began to stir.

"Lady Edith!" he said again.

"E…dith," the woman mumbled.

"Lady Edith, you need to pray!"

"P-p-pray," she muttered.

"You need to wake up and pray!"

"P-pray…mmumf…pray f-for…"

"YES!" Creedle said enthusiastically when he saw that it was working.

"Pray for y-yes," the elderly woman muttered.

"NO!" Creedle corrected.

"No," Edith murmured and shook her head slightly.

The little angel tried again.

"Lady Edith, you must pray for your grandson! You must pray for Blake Miller!"

"Pray for Blakey," she repeated.

"Yes, Lady Edith! Wake up and pray for Blakey. He's in trouble and needs your prayers! Wake up, Lady Edith, wake up!"

Suddenly Edith's eyes flew open, and she sat up stiffly. She looked around the room with a confused look. A sudden light of determined purpose shown in her eyes, and she slid off her bed and onto her knees. The little angel clapped his hands with delight.

"Hello, my sweet Father in heaven!" she prayed cheerfully. "I know we talked just before I laid down to take my nap, but I feel a strong urgency to pray for my Blakey. I don't know what might be happening, but I lift my grandson up to you again, Father.

"You have all power and might at Your disposal! You have all authority over everyone and everything! Oh, sweet Lord, if Blake's in trouble, You are his only hope! Since he has gotten older, he's turned away from You and resisted whenever I've tried to point him to Your amazing love for him. But Father, I know that You love him! You love him enough to offer Your Son on a cross for him! I also know that it's Your will to save him, because Your word tells me that You are not willing that any should perish but that all should come to repentance! That's Your will, Father, and You know it's my will also, so I'm joining my will with Yours, and I'm asking You to send Your awesome power...the power that raised Jesus from the dead...the power that seated Jesus at your right hand....far above all rule and authority and power and dominion...now and forever, and deliver my Blakey from whatever he's gotten himself into and please bring him to faith in Your wonderful Son!"

Edith was just getting warmed up. "Oh sweet, wonderful, and amazing Father in Heaven, what a privilege it is to know You and to pray in Your power..."

It thrilled Creedle to listen to this great lover of his Master pour out her heart in faith and love for her grandson. He wanted to stay and hear more, but he had done his job, and now he desperately needed to get back and help his companions with the battle.

Pulling out the glowing disc, he saw the image of Lady Edith on her knees praying to God on one side. Flipping it over, he saw an image of Tirian with his sword drawn on the other. "HA!" Creedle exclaimed as he realized how to return to his companions.

Holding that side up, the small angel cried, "TO TIRIAN!" He instantly shot out of the room like a bullet out of a gun.

Unaware of what was happening in the spirit world around her, Edith Miller continued to cry out in her simple faith for the safety, protection, and salvation of her grandson.

Suddenly the courageous little warrior of God was back with his friends. "Hey, guys, did you miss me?"

"Creedle!" Tirian cried when he heard his small friend's voice. "I was hoping you'd stay with Lady Edith...out of danger!"

"Now that wouldn't have been any fun," Creedle answered with a chuckle. "I see those black-hearted buzzards have just about doubled their numbers in the couple of minutes that I've been gone."

"It's going to be bad," Barcos announced.

"They'll be dropping on us any second now," Tirian said, staring at the horde hovering above the racing ambulance. "Were you able to get Lady Edith praying?"

"*Hee, hee.* What do you think?" the small angel said with a laugh. "Can't you feel it?"

A surge of power began to move up through their angelic bodies, and the celestial light that emanated from them and their weapons began to glow brighter and brighter.

"YES!" Barcos roared, feeling the growing strength in his body. Determinedly he gripped his sword tighter as all three, with their new power swelling in them, viewed the coming battle with eagerness.

"OH, THE POWER OF A PRAYER WARRIOR!" Tirian roared as he swung his great sword around his head effortlessly.

All of the demons saw what was happening below them and were reluctant to begin the attack.

"There's only three of them," the boss encouraged his fighters, "really only two and a half."

"But they're getting' power from somewhere, boss!" one of the warriors called out with concern. "The light coming from them is getting brighter and brighter!"

"Well then, hurry up and go get 'em before they get any stronger!" the boss ordered. "ATTACK!"

Screaming their demonic cries, the hovering dark horde dropped like an avalanche on the three defenders. The closer the demons came, the brighter the light grew that radiated from the angels. The power in the angels was so strong that the enemy warriors could feel its buzz through their bodies as they drew near. At that moment the fierce war cries of the demons began to turn into cries of terror. Glowing balls of fire zipped from Creedle's sling, diminishing the numbers of demons before they even arrived.

When the mass of enemy fighters slammed into the two super powerful angels, Tirian and Barcos didn't budge an inch. With booming cries of "FOR THE KING OF GLORY," the two angelic warriors began deflecting descending sword blades and slashing great gaps through the army of darkness. Creedle, hovering behind his two friends, continued to rapidly sling accurate missiles of radiant light balls into the attacking army.

Huge clouds of black, steamy smoke began to boil up from the clashing blades as gashed, slashed, and stricken demons began to deflate and wither to the ground. On the fierce battle continued as the warriors of light protected Miller.

Interestingly, while the screams of the demons, the war cries, and the noise of the battle was almost deafening to the angels in the fight, the emergency medical crew in the ambulance tending to Blake Miller was completely oblivious to the intense spiritual conflict going on right over their heads.

"He's starting to calm down!" one of the EMTs said to the other. "The sedative seems to be working."

"Whew, yeah," the other agreed, having just completed an exam on Blake's vital signs. "That was really intense, but he seems to be stable and resting for the moment."

"Good," the first one acknowledged as the fierce battle continued over their heads. "After this crazy day, maybe we will have a nice, peaceful ride back to the hospital."

Chapter Twenty-Two

Chapter Twenty-Three

All Blake knew was blackness. He seemed to be floating in some different dark world. In the back of his mind, he was aware that an unspeakable evil was coming and wanted to destroy him.

He thought he heard something, and his body turned involuntarily. As it did so, he could see a small light in the distance, and he was drawn uncontrollably towards it.

The closer he drew to the light, it became bigger and brighter. Also he noticed that his left arm and his abdomen began to feel sore. The nearer he got to the light, the more intense the pain became. Even so, he could not stop approaching the radiance, nor did he want to. Something or someone was calling him.

Just then he opened his eyes and saw a face he didn't recognize, and she smiled at him. "You need to wake up, sleepy head," the woman's voice said cheerfully.

Blake blinked twice and tried to focus on the face.

"Hey, Blake," she said louder, "can you hear me?"

Miller nodded his head, and his eyes got wide as he looked anxiously around the room.

"Just be calm," she said, noticing his agitation. "Everything is okay."

Blake began breathing rapidly as he continued to search the room. "Where are they? Are…are they here?" he asked, beginning to panic. "ARE THEY HERE?"

"There's nothing to worry about, Blake," the woman answered with a smile and placed a hand on his shoulder. "There's no one in the room but people who care about you. Look over there by the window. There's your grandmother."

Blake's eyes cut across the room, and he saw Edith Miller sitting beside it, her swollen eyes red and wet.

"NANA!" he cried and reached for her.

Edith jumped from her seat and rushed to give her injured grandson a very gentle hug. Blake buried his head in his grandmother's shoulder and sobbed.

After several long minutes Blake pulled back and looked seriously at his grandmother. "Nana, the demons…they're real, and they want to get me!"

Edith smiled and said with confidence, "They'll have to get through me."

Blake gave a weak smiled and said, "You sound like a friend of mine."

"Do you remember what happened, Blakey?" Edith asked.

"I was in a plane crash."

"Yes, that's right," Edith said nervously. "It was a really bad crash, Blakey. I hate to have to tell you this, but everyone else…"

"I know, Nana," Blake interrupted sadly. "They all died."

"You were in pretty bad shape when they brought you in," the nurse volunteered. "You have lots of bruises, scrapes, and cuts all over. You also sustained multiple fractures in your left arm and hand that needed surgery, but your most serious injury was a torn spleen.

"Your seat tearing loose from the plane actually saved you, but when you hit the ground, the seatbelt jerked so hard against your abdomen that it ruptured your spleen. It's a good thing they got you here as soon as they did!"

"That's why I have this bandage on my belly," Blake reasoned. "Did they have to sew up my spleen?"

"They removed it," the nurse answered.

"Wait…WHAT? They removed my spleen! Can you do that?"

"It's okay," the nurse reassured him. "You can live just fine without your spleen. It's just a bag that stores extra blood when you need it, and helps in fighting infections. My brother-in-law lost his spleen twelve years ago and is doing fine."

"So what does not having one mean?" Blake asked with concern.

"It only means that, if you get an infection, we will have to watch it carefully and start antibiotics quickly if we need to.

"All that happened two days ago," the nurse continued.

"We tried to wake you up soon after the surgery, but you screamed and fought terribly. It was so bad that we had to sedate you again. The doctors figured that it was the pain you were feeling. Today we allowed you to wake up gradually, and you've done better."

"It wasn't the pain," Blake answered. "It was fear."

"Fear?" the nurse asked.

"It was awful!" the patient said with a shiver. "I've been through hell…literally!

"You prayed for me, didn't you Nana?"

"I always pray for you, Blakey."

"But you said a special prayer for me this time. I know you did."

Edith gave her grandson a sideways look before she answered, "It was the funniest thing. Two days ago I was taking an afternoon nap, and I went from being sound asleep to sitting straight up in bed. I don't know what happened, but when I woke up, I had such a strong urge to pray for you…"

"Your prayers saved my life, Nana…more than once. I'll tell you all about it later. " He reached up with his good arm, and his grandmother leaned into another long hug.

"Thank you for praying for me," he said earnestly in her ear. "Thank you, thank you, thank you!"

Looking past his grandmother, Blake noticed a familiar-looking man sitting near the window.

"I know you," Blake said weakly as he made eye contact with the man.

"Uh…yes…yes, we've met before," the man nervously returned.

"This is Brother Jeff Simms, my minister," Edith reminded him. "You remember Brother Jeff from when you came by for my birthday."

"Oh, yeah," Blake returned with a nod. "I…uh…remember I cussed you out that day."

"Well, yes," Jeff returned nervously, "but I had no right to try to talk to you about spiritual things without your permission.

"So…uh…I'm so glad that you are alive!"

Jeff shifted uncomfortably, looked at Edith, and gave her a nod. "Listen," he said to both of them, "I don't want to interfere with your time together, so…uh…I'll think I'll just leave you two alone."

"WAIT!" Blake almost shouted with a wild look in his eyes. "DON'T GO! YOU CAN'T GO!

"NANA, DON'T LET HIM GO!"

"Just calm down, Blake," the nurse said with concern when she saw the change in him. "You need to rest."

"It's alright, Blakey," Edith said, patting his hand and nodding reassuringly at the concerned nurse. "I'm sure that Brother Jeff can stay a few more minutes if it's important to you. Isn't that right, Bother Jeff?"

The surprised minister nodded his willingness to remain.

"Good! Good!" Miller said with relief. "Nana, I need you to pray over me right now like you've never prayed before!"

"Sure," she answered calmly. "I'll pray for you."

"I mean serious, powerful prayers, Nana!"

"Okay, sweetheart, I will pray hard, but what's wrong?"

"Satan wants me in the worst way!" Blake exclaimed. Edith and Jeff looked at each other.

"You can't see it," Blake said urgently, "but they're fighting over me RIGHT NOW! Nana, you've got to keep them away from me while I talk to this man."

Looking at the minister, Blake said, "Brother Jack?"

"Jeff."

"JEFF...sorry. I need you to talk to me about Jesus and how to get saved."

Jeff was stunned. "Uh...well, okay then! I can do that. So, Blake, I want you to repeat this prayer after me."

"Hold it!" Blake shot back. "Are there examples of people in the Bible who got saved?"

"Well...sure," Jeff answered a little confused. "There are lots of examples in the book of Acts."

Chapter Twenty-Three

"So, how many of those people got saved by saying your prayer?"

"Uh…hmm…well, I guess none of them."

"No disrespect to your prayer," Blake returned, "but this is serious to me, and I've got to be sure. I want you to give it to me straight. Don't tell me what you think. Show me straight out of the Bible. Do you understand? I need to see it in the Bible. And don't beat around the bush. Cut to the chase! Give me the short and to-the-point version. I need Him RIGHT NOW!"

"Bother Jeff," Edith said as she paused her prayer, "start with Acts two, and then show him chapters eight, nine, ten, sixteen, and twenty-two."

"Yes, ma'am."

Chapter Twenty-Four

Another especially beautiful place in Paradise was what everyone called the King's flower garden. Milton was surprised at how vast it was. Actually, he was impressed with how large and expansive everything was in Heaven. Everyone dearly loved this particular garden, so Jesus had made it immense enough for multitudes of people to enjoy it at the same time without being crowded.

Milton had been drawn to a large, open part of the garden by the music. A great crowd was there listening to hundreds of followers of Jesus from the nations of Iran and Iraq, two countries who had fought bitter wars against each other, singing worship songs to God with all their might. They wore their traditional dress costumes and started out in two separate groups, singing about all that had divided their nations on earth. But then the song became really exciting as they began singing about the walls that Jesus had broken down and the unity that all people have in Christ Jesus. Just then angels appeared, playing harps, horns, pipes, tambourines, and other instruments that Milton had never seen before. As the angelic orchestra joined in, all the singers began to dance as they sang. Eventually they moved back and forth until the two groups joined together. Then with their arms across each other's shoulders, their song told of the deep and passionate love of Jesus that bound them all together as one. When the chorus of the song began again in power, everyone in the large audience began singing with them. Milton was stunned that he also knew the song and sang it with all his heart, even though this was the first time he had heard it.

As they sang it again, everyone who wasn't playing an instrument put their arms around those singing beside them and caroled in passionate worship about the wonderful, uniting love of Jesus.

The colorful birds above the singers began to fly and soar in rhythm with the moving song. Even the fountains in the nearby ponds and pools shot up geysers like liquid fireworks to join in the worship.

Milton had never in his life experienced anything so wonderful! He was moved to worship the Father and His amazing Son with all his heart. Seeing the unity and love expressed by the two nations of former enemies, Milton was also moved to love everyone who loved Jesus Christ even more deeply.

Afterwards Milton walked up to a small group of the singers. They immediately pulled him into their group and began introducing themselves. They were each eager to hear Milton's story on how he learned to love the Lord Jesus. It both stunned and humbled him to find out that many of his new Iranian and Iraqi friends had been killed in the shadow world because of their faith in Jesus. Milton tried to show these martyrs great honor and respect, but they acted like their sacrifices were nothing.

Quite a while later Milton was strolling through a vast field of the most glorious flowers he had ever seen. The fragrances were magnificent, and he absolutely loved breathing in the amazing scents.

Just then he heard a sweet voice behind him say, "Son of Compassion."

Turning, Milton saw Jesus. "Oh, Your Majesty!" Milton said with surprise. "I'm so glad to see You again. These flowers are amazing! Have you smelled…?"

The smile on Jesus's face stopped Milton mid-sentence. "Oh…yeah," Milton said sheepishly. "I guess you have."

"They are wonderful, aren't they?" Jesus said.

Milton nodded his head as Jesus looked thoughtfully at him. "You're concerned about Carol," the Lord said knowingly.

"She saw the awful me," Milton answered sadly. "It was really bad for her, Jesus; all the drunkenness, drugs and my selfishness. After I found You, I never got the chance to talk to her before I…uh…you know…had to leave."

"What do you want for Carol?" Jesus asked.

"Oh, I really want her to know about You and to be able to come here! I also want her to not be sad about me dying. I know how she is, Jesus. She's going to think that somehow my death is her fault."

"Why don't we go see how she's doing?" Jesus suggested.

"What? Can we do that?"

"Sure," the King returned with a smile. "Almost everyone here has people still in the shadow world they are concerned about. How do you think Michael and Trudy kept up with you? Come with me."

Jesus led Milton out of the flower garden and along one of the golden streets until they came to a beautiful, opal-paved walkway. The plants and flowers lining the path were gorgeous and fragrant.

"Is this another garden?" Milton asked.

Jesus laughed and said, "Dear friend, everything here is a garden! Do you see that running water flowing beside the path? Well, that is a tributary of the River of Life. It flows into the ivory palace you see just ahead."

As they entered the grand mansion, Jesus pointed out the living water that flowed through the middle of the magnificent structure and into a very large, crystal clear pool in the center of the vast room.

There were ornately carved ivory benches all around the water, and Milton noticed that a large number of people were standing or sitting beside the water. He saw that every one of them seemed to be staring intensely into the clear waters of the pool.

"Even though you are here in Paradise," Jesus said, "the Father and I love it when the Spirit of Truth brings us your prayers. You have seen that the Holy Spirit has remained with you here as well.

"Whenever you feel Carol or other friends you left behind pulling at your heart, you may come here. Ask the Spirit to show you the ones you are curious about, and if the Father is willing, you will see and possibly hear them. But, Milton, do not expect to be able to communicate with them. Present your petitions for them to your Father and Me. The Holy Spirit will bring your prayers to Us instantly, and We will hear and always respond to you."

Milton nodded his understanding and turned to face the pure, clear waters of the large pool. "Spirit of God," he began, "may I please see Carol Collins?"

"Yes," said a sweet voice in Milton's ear, and immediately lights began to swirl in the water in front of him.

"There she is," Milton said excitedly as he viewed the moving image in the pool. "This is like television! She's crying, Lord! I knew something was wrong. Where is she?"

"She's at the visitation before your funeral," Jesus answered.

"Whoa!" Milton shot back. "Have I been here that long?"

"There is no time here, my dear friend," the King answered. "I can show you your birth, your life, or your death as they actually happen. You were concerned about how Carol is handling your death, and that can best be seen at your funeral."

"Listen to her, Jesus! She keeps saying that she's sorry and that she should have been a better wife to me. It's just like I said! She thinks my death is somehow her fault! She was a great wife to me, and there is no way that me dying in a plane crash was her fault!"

"She could have been a better wife if she had known Me," the King countered, "but she didn't. Given that, she did the best she knew to do. Now Milton, this is not for your entertainment. Consider carefully. What does Carol need, and what can you do to help her?"

"Most importantly," Milton answered, "she needs You, Your Majesty. And she needs to know that I'm doing great. Would you do those things for her, please?"

"I have heard you, My friend," Jesus answered with a smile. "Now watch how I answer your request."

As Milton observed his ex-wife sobbing beside the closed casket, a couple walked up to her.

"Hey!" Milton exclaimed. "That's Scott and his wife, Phyllis! They taught me about You, Your Majesty!"

"They loved you," Jesus said, "and they've come to the funeral to show their respects and to minister in My name."

Chapter Twenty-Five

Carol Collins didn't think her life could get any worse — but it had. Milton's depression, laced with all of his drug and alcohol addictions, had broken her. She had loved Milton, but Carol was no saint. When it had escalated and reached her breaking point, she took the only option she felt she had and left him.

Rather than giving her a sense of relief or freedom, the divorce had left her empty and feeling like a failure. She had thought that, if Milt could just get free from the drugs and alcohol, maybe they could get back together. But now, standing in front of his coffin, she felt that her hopes and her life were totally and completely crushed.

She hadn't even been able to say goodbye to Milton. She hadn't seen him after the plane crash. The mortician said that, between the crash and the fire, there really wasn't much of his body left. They had to identify him by his dental records.

"Milton…Milton, I'm so sorry! If only I had been more patient with you," she sobbed out loud. "If only I had been a better wife and tried harder to understand how you felt, maybe…"

"Are you Carol?"

The voice startled the grieving woman, and she turned to see who had spoken. Standing before her was a big man with a scruffy, greying beard and kind eyes. Beside him was a small woman with such a look of compassion on her face that Carol instantly felt drawn to her.

"Yes," she sniffed, "I'm Carol. Who are you?"

"I'm Scott Jones, and this is my wife, Phyllis," the man returned. "We were friends of Milton."

With effort Carol showed the couple polite interest that she did not feel at the time. "How did you know Milt?"

"Milton and I worked together at the state garage."

"Oh," Carol said remembering, "I think I remember Milt mentioning your name."

"When we realized that Milton was having problems," Scott continued, "Phyllis and I reached out to him. We actually became quite good friends over the last couple of months."

"Carol," Phyllis began taking up the narrative, "Milton opened up to us and told us about all his failures and how he had hurt his relationship with you. He told us how he wanted to change and try to make things right with you."

Tears streamed down Carol's guarded face as she heard Phyllis's words.

"He was serious about changing," Scott added. "He knew he couldn't do it alone, so he joined himself to the only Person Who could give him a new life."

"Who was that?" Carol asked with a confused look on her face.

"He became a follower of Jesus Christ," Scott answered. "Phyllis and I and a few others had the privilege of studying the Bible with Milton to help him start becoming the man he wanted to be."

"Milt became a Christian?" the grieving woman asked in shock. "Milton Collins?"

"He did," Scott answered, "just a few weeks ago. He wanted you to know and tried to call and tell you about his faith, but he couldn't reach you."

"I remember his calls," Carol said, dropping her eyes. "I was still hurting and didn't answer."

"Well, one of the last things he said to Phyllis and me was that he was not going to give up on trying to make things right with you, whether you forgave him or not."

"And you think Milton was serious about changing?"

"Carol," Phyllis answered, "he wasn't just serious, he was doing it. With Christ's help he had completely given up the drugs and the alcohol. He started going with us to church and came every time the doors were open."

"We had him in our home twice a week just to study the Bible," Scott said. "He constantly had questions. It was like, once he believed in Jesus, he wanted to learn everything he could about Him."

"You're both telling me that my husband, Milton Collins, gave up his drugs and alcohol and became a dedicated Christian?"

"I think you would have been proud of the man he was becoming," Phyllis said with a smile.

All of this stunned Carol, and spotting a seat nearby, she walked over and sat down to consider what Scott and Phyllis had told her.

"I can't believe that, after the way he lived his life, Milt became a..a Christian!" Quickly looking into the eyes of her new friends, Carol asked earnestly, "So Milt's probably in heaven?"

"I guarantee it!" Scott said with a big grin. "Most likely he's looking down on us right this minute."

Now Carol cried again, but this time they were tears of relief. Phyllis walked over and put her arm around the tearful woman.

"If it would be okay with you," Scott continued, "Phyllis and I would like to remain with you for the rest of the visitation and the funeral to follow."

Carol looked up at Scott and grabbed Phyllis's hand and nodded yes.

"Then afterwards," Phyllis added, "we want you to come by the house for supper. Scott and I have so much we want to tell you about the good man your husband had become and about the One Who brought the change into his life."

Chapter Twenty-Five

Chapter Twenty-Six

Blake Miller sat in a wheel chair in the garden courtyard just outside the hospital's cafeteria. He was surrounded by a small crowd of enthralled listeners. They included eight nurses, six patients, two drug salesmen, and a janitor on break. All of them were mesmerized by the fascinating story that Blake had spent the last forty minutes telling them.

"And you believe all of that," one of the nurses asked as he finished his narrative, "the demons, the pit of fire, the angels, the silver cord…all of it?"

"Yep," Miller said with a smile. "I tried not to, but I couldn't help myself. When I was convinced that the demons were real, of course that meant that God and Jesus were real as well. Being convinced of the bad, I had to run to the good."

"But you were unconscious," another nurse added. "Couldn't it have been a dream?"

"Not from my view," Blake answered. "The fact that I was unconscious proves that it wasn't a dream."

"What do you mean?" the nurse questioned.

"I know too many of the details of what actually happened. I couldn't have known them if I hadn't been watching it."

"And you think that it was your grandmother's prayers that saved you?" the janitor asked.

"Oh, there's no doubt in my mind about that!" Blake said confidently. "Even the angels couldn't have kept the demons from destroying me without the power of her prayers!

"I was one lost, pathetic person," Blake said unashamedly, "but my Nana's a warrior for Christ, and she never quit going to battle for me! Even when I rejected her attempts to get me to see the truth and made fun of her, she continued to pray for me. All the angels know her! They call her Lady Edith, and when she prays, the angels get awesome power!"

"She sounds wonderful," a nurse said. "I'd like to meet her.

"So would I," said another.

"That's no problem," Blake said with a smile. "That's her sitting on the bench over there."

Everyone turned to look.

"What's she doing over there?" one of the patients asked. "I thought she would be over here with you, helping to tell what happened."

"Well, Satan hates it when I tell this story and explain my faith in Jesus Christ," Blake answered. "Nana and I discovered that more people listen when she prays while I talk. We figure that her prayer cover keeps the demons at bay.

"Hey, Nana!" Blake called. "I've finished my story, and these people want to meet you. Can you come over here for a minute?"

The older saint smiled as she rose to her feet and made her way to the small crowd. She shook all of their hands and took the time to ask each one their names. A few of them asked her to pray for them. Several of the listeners had to ask her questions subtly verifying the accuracy of what Blake had said.

As they talked, someone approached from behind. "Blake Miller?" a voice said, and a man in a uniform stepped up to the recovering patient.

"Yes," Blake returned nervously when he saw the officer.

"They told me at the nurse's station that you were out here. I'm Deputy Randell Phelps."

"Yes, I remember you, Deputy Phelps!" Blake said enthusiastically. "You found me at the plane crash! Thank you for what you did for me!" Blake stuck out his good hand to shake the deputy's.

"Actually," Phelps returned with a smile, "it's not me who deserves your thanks. It's this guy." With his left hand Phelps pulled gently on a leash, and a thin, rough-looking beagle limped in front of Blake.

"Is this the dog you said saved you?" one of the nurses gasped.

"Yep, that's him!" Blake beamed. "I'm so glad he's alive! I thought he must have died from the snake bite."

Deputy Phelps stood there with a stunned look on his face. "Sorry, but I'm kind of confused. You were unconscious, so how did you know about the dog or the snake?"

"I was on the other side of the veil watching," Miller said offhandedly.

"What veil?"

"There's a veil between life and death," Blake answered. "Because I was closer to death than life at the time, my conscious self was on the other side of the veil watching all that you and this little guy were doing."

"He also saw what the demons were doing," one of the nurses added.

"Demons?" Phelps asked with a confused look.

"And the angels!" asserted the janitor.

"Well, ahhh, all I know is that this little dog was amazing!" Phelps said to Blake. "Even after getting snake bit and in terrible pain, he would not leave you. He howled and howled until he got our attention. He was so loyal that at first I thought he must be your dog, but when I saw what kind of shape he was in, it was clear that he had been on his own for quite some time.

"After we got you in the ambulance, I went back to check on the dog. By that time his leg, neck, and head were terribly swollen from the snake venom. It was so bad that he was starting to have trouble breathing. I didn't think he could last much longer, so I put him in my cruiser, and with my lights on and siren screaming, I rushed him to Auburn's vet school.

"I radioed in that I was bringing him, and a bunch of doctors and vet students were waiting for him when I pulled up. They took him in and started to work.

"When everyone at the station found out what the little beagle did, we all chipped in to get him fixed up. I made sure the vet school knew that he was a hero as well, and they did a lot of the work on him for free. As you can see, they did a great job.

"As soon as he's a little better, we'll put him up for adoption."

"That won't be necessary," Blake said. "After all he's done for me…he's family.

"Nana, can you take care of him until I get out of the hospital?"

"Of course, dear," Edith returned with a smile as she bent down to rub the dog's ears. The short beagle in turn licked her hand in appreciation.

"You'll have to come up with a name for him," Phelps said as he handed Edith the leash.

"Well, it was his persistent barking that saved my life," Blake reasoned, "so I think I'll call him Barkos—after a friend of mine."

Blake reached down with his good arm and scratched Barkos's head lovingly. As he did so, an idea came to him. "We'll be a team, Nana!" Blake said excitedly. "Whenever I get a chance to tell my adventure on how I came to faith in Jesus, you pray, I'll talk, and Barkos will be my visual aid."

"So, you're going to start a ministry?" one of the nurses asked.

"Is God calling you to be a preacher?" the janitor probed.

"What? No!" Blake shot back, laughing. "But Jesus *has* worked in my life, and I'm going to tell people about it. You know He's working in your lives as well. So look for what He's doing and tell people. They need to know."

The End

Chapter Twenty-Six

<u>Appendix</u>

A good story not only entertains you, it should also challenge you to be a better person and make you think higher thoughts. God our Father in the Old Testament and Jesus Christ in the New Testament both used stories to teach important spiritual lessons. It has been discovered that whenever an engaging story is used to instruct, the lessons bypass the cerebral cortex, where short term memory is located, and go straight to the hippocampus in the brain, where long term memory occurs. By using exciting stories, teachers have the potential to place the lessons directly into the long term memories of their students.

For this reason I want to encourage readers to consider using my stories to teach. To do that I am including chapter questions in this appendix to assist in promoting meaningful discussions. These questions are just suggestions. You may be able to think of some better ones or questions that better fit your group. It is not important to cover all the questions. The important part is to encourage each other to know Christ better, to draw near to God, and to follow Christ more effectively through your discussions.

CHAPTER ONE

How does a person get a reputation like Scott?

Why do you think Milton and Carol are having problems in their marriage?

What could they do to help build a healthy relationship?

What is unhealthy about the way Milton sees himself?

What does God's word say about handling finances? (*Proverbs 6: 1-11; 10:2-5; 11: 18, 24-28; 12:11, 24; 21:17; 22:9*)

What godly character qualities would help Milton and Carol?

CHAPTER TWO

What determines whether a decision is wise or foolish?

What does it take for a person to make a wise decision?

Do you think Jeff Simms was right or wrong to push Blake into a conversation about his soul?

Jesus said, "*No one can come to the Father unless the Father Who sent Me draws him.*" What are some signs that God might be drawing a person to Himself?

CHAPTER THREE

Milton has problems with alcohol, drugs, and handling money, but what are his root problems?

Why is it so hard for Milton to say 'no' to temptations?

How did Scott show Jesus to Milton?

What must take place in a person's life for genuine change to occur?

What did it take in your life for you to make Jesus your King?

CHAPTER FOUR

Come up with a good definition of a true friend.

What character qualities and traits do you consider to be important for a good friend to have?

How would you describe the friendship between David and Jonathan? (*I Samuel 18:1-4; I Samuel 19:1-6; I Samuel 20:12-17*)

Both John and Judas were considered by Jesus to be his friends. How would you compare the friendship of each?

When Milton was an unbeliever, the difficulties and pressures of life motivated him to choose alcohol, drugs, and withdrawal as a way to cope. How could faith in Jesus have helped him at that time?

CHAPTER FIVE

What actually is death?

Why is the idea of dying so scary to people?

How did Milton's experience differ from that of his friends?

Some people don't believe hell is real. What was Jesus's view of hell? (*Matthew 5:22, 29-30; Luke 12:4-5; Luke 16:22-28*)

Some people don't believe demons are real. What was Jesus's view of demons? (*Luke 11:17-26*)

What does the Bible say happens to believers in Jesus when they die? (*Luke 23: 42-43; Philippians 1:21-24*)

What are some of the promises God makes to His followers who are faithful until death? (*Revelation 2:10; Hebrew 10:35-36; I Peter 1:6-9; II Timothy 4:7-8*)

CHAPTER SIX

Some people don't believe in Paradise or heaven. What is Jesus's view of Paradise? (*Luke 23: 39-43*)

Someone has said that, without Jesus, heaven would be hell. Do you think that is true?

What is Jesus's purpose in giving gifts to us? (*I Peter 4:11, Ephesians 4:7-14*)

Do you think there will be much joy in Paradise when someone finally makes it home to Heaven?

What will it take in a person's life here on earth for them to hear Jesus say, 'Well done good and faithful servant,' when they stand before Christ?

What are some of the things the Holy Spirit does for the followers of Jesus as they live out their faith on the earth? (*Romans 8:16, 26-27; Ephesians 1:13-14; I John 4:13; 16:13; Galatians 5:22-23*)

How does the Bible describe Paradise? (*Luke 16:22-25; Revelation 4 and 21*)

CHAPTER SEVEN

What is faith?

Since the demons believe that Jesus is God's Son but they are not saved, describe the kind of faith that does produce salvation.

What does the Bible say about the power of faith? (*Matthew 17:20, Hebrew 11*)

What does the Bible say about the power of prayer? (*James 5:13-18*)

How does God feel about our prayers? (*I John 5:14, Hebrews 4:14-16, Matthew 7:7-11*)

Name some times in the Bible when faithful prayer changed things. (*Acts 4:24-31, 12:5-11; I Kings 20:18-46*)

Describe some times in your life when faithful prayer has changed things.

CHAPTER EIGHT

How does God describe the spiritual state of a person who does not believe in Jesus? (*Romans 1:18-32; II Corinthians 4:3-4, 6:14-18*)

What is the best that an unbeliever can hope for in this life?

Define the kind of hope that God gives?

What do the followers of Jesus hope for? (*Romans 8:20-21; Colossians 1:3-5, 24-27; Acts 24:14-15*)

For the child of God, when will hope end?
(*Romans 8:24-25, Revelation 2:10*)

When will faith end?

When will love end?

CHAPTER NINE

Jesus said '*…I am with you always, even to the end of the world.*' What does that mean to followers of Jesus?

What is each person worth to God?

Have you ever experienced Jesus calling you or reaching out to you?

In John 6:44 Jesus said, '*No one can come to the Father unless the Father Who sent Me draws him.*' How does God draw people to Himself?

Is it God's will for sinful people to perish in hell? (*II Peter 3:9*)

What good reasons could God have for allowing us to face difficult situations?

What is God's ultimate goal for us? (*I John 3:1-2, John 17:3, 11, 22-24*)

CHAPTER TEN

Did God create Hell for the purpose of punishing sinful people? (*Matthew 25:41*)

What does God say Hell is like? (*Matthew 25:41, 46; Mark 9:43; Revelation 20:10*)

Did God allow certain people to be born specifically so He could throw them in Hell? (*II Peter 3:9*)

What can a sinful person do to change their eternal destiny? (*Acts 2:37-38*)

What happens when a person calls on the name of Jesus for help? (*Romans 10:8-9*)

What can the prayers of a righteous person accomplish? (*James 5:16-18*)

Why should a follower of Jesus not fear Satan or his demons?

CHAPTER ELEVEN

Give examples of lies that Satan successfully tells people today.

Why do people believe Satan's lies?

Why is it critically important to identify the lies Satan tells and reject them?

According to the Bible, why is it important to know the truth? (*John 8:32*)

Do you agree that the servants of Satan don't have to work very hard in North America to trap the souls of people? Explain your answer.

What are some of the things that suppress and quench a passion for Christ in this country?

From where does a passion for following Jesus Christ come? (*Titus 2:11-14; Matthew 7:7-11*)

Why do many Christians resist or avoid praying together?

CHAPTER TWELVE

In the story the angels used the name of Jesus like a weapon. What does the Bible say about the power in the name of Jesus? (*John 14:13-14; Mark 16:17-18; Philippians 2:8-11*)

How are the followers of Jesus to use His name? (*Mark 16:17-18; Acts 16:18; Acts 4:30: Proverbs 18:10*)

What effect does the name of Jesus have on Satan and that which is evil? (*Mark 16:17-18; Philippians 2:9-11*)

Have any of you called out to Jesus for help? What was the result?

In what ways have you been a witness of God's faithfulness in your life?

What are the blessings and benefits of believing in God's faithfulness?

CHAPTER THIRTEEN

The characters in the story refer to the earth and the world we live in as the shadow world and it refers to us as shadowlanders. What do you think is meant by that? (*Hebrews 8:5, 10:1; Colossians 2:16-17; Matthew 4:16; John 8:12*)

How does knowing that we live in a world that is simply a shadow of the one to come help prepare us for that new world?

What did you learn about Jesus in the World Room of Lampstands?

What does it take for a church's lampstand to be cast out?

What part can you play in helping your church's lampstand to shine brightly?

What can you do or fail to do that will quench the light of Christ?

What kind of religion is a burden to Jesus? (*Matthew 7:21-23, 23:13-28*)

CHAPTER FOURTEEN

How devastating is hopelessness to the human heart?

How do people respond to hopelessness?

How does Jesus provide hope for His followers?

Describe the response Jesus wants His followers to have in difficult, scary, or seemingly "hopeless" situations. (*Proverbs 3:3-6; Matthew 6:25-33, 7:7-8*)

You can find the story of Shadrack, Meshack, Abednego, and the fiery furnace in Daniel 3. What motivated such courage and faithfulness in these men?

Why does God sometimes do good things for bad people? (*Romans 2:4*)

What is God's ultimate goal in the things He does and allows in our lives? (*John 17:1-3; Romans 1:19-20; Acts 17:27; Psalm 19:1-4*)

Why is it important that God give people a choice to love Him or not?

CHAPTER FIFTEEN

What lies does Satan tell sinful people who really want to change their lives, and why do they believe those lies?

Where does the power to live a righteous and holy life come from? (*Titus 2:11-14*)

In Philippians 2:13 the Bible says that God is at work in you both to will and to work for His good pleasure. This means that God's grace in us not only motivates us to desire His will but also gives us the power to do His will. What does that mean for your life?

What are some things you are powerless to do that God can give you the power to accomplish for His glory?

What must you do to get that power? (*Proverbs 3:3-6; Matthew 7:7-11*)

Jesus tells us in Matthew 6:33 that we are to seek first the kingdom of God and His righteousness. What would doing that look like in your everyday life?

Why does God ask us to live a life that only His power in us can accomplish?

CHAPTER SIXTEEN

Describe the difference between how a believer in Jesus Christ and an unbeliever view death.

Describe a time when you followed your will instead of God's will. How did it turn out?

Describe a time when you followed God's will instead of your will. How did it turn out?

How does a follower of Jesus view God's will?

Describe the difference between trusting daily in Jesus and trusting in yourself.

What effect will faithfully trusting daily in Jesus have on your life?

How much does Satan want you to be lost?

How much does God want you to be saved?

CHAPTER SEVENTEEN

What kind of things do you think you will learn in Heaven?

In John 17:3 Jesus said that eternal life was knowing God and Himself. Generally speaking, how do you think the Father and Jesus will reveal to us more and more about themselves?

What are some of the amazing things God has already shown you personally about His power, love, and faithfulness?

What can you learn about God when you look deeply at the stars? The ocean? A blue whale? A honey bee?

How has God shown what He's like in people you know?

How is the Lord Jesus revealing His holy nature in you?

What are some things that prevent God's Spirit from revealing Himself through you?

CHAPTER EIGHTEEN

The providence of God is seen when things happen to us, seemingly by chance, that turn out to be great blessings. Do you know of times when God's providence was evident?

How has God shown you His providence?

Can you think of some of God's promises that give you confidence to face difficult times? (*James 4:6-8, 10; II Thessalonians 3:3*)

What are God's purposes for making promises to us? (*II Peter 1:3-11*)

Share details of how God has kept His promises in your life.

Describe what someone's life would be like if they could not count on God's promises.

What are the benefits to knowing that God's promises are for you and that He will always keep them?

CHAPTER NINETEEN

Can you think of times in the Bible when Satan interfered with God's work? (*Genesis 3; Daniel 10; II Corinthians 4:3-4; Matthew 4:3-10*)

When did God defeat Satan? (*Genesis 3:15; Colossians 2:13-15*)

Why do you think God allows Satan to continue to work evil on earth?

What ultimately is going to happen to Satan and his demons?

When Satan comes against us, what does God want us to do? (*James 4:7-8*)

How does God use Satan's attacks for our good?

Satan's primary power is to lie and deceive. How is the best way to overcome Satan's lies? (*Ephesians 6:13-18; Matthew 4:3-10*)

CHAPTER TWENTY

Why do you think the angels used "*For the King of Glory*" as their battle cry?

What does it mean to serve the King of Glory?

Daniel chapter 10 describes interactions between angels and demons. What can you learn about the spiritual realm from reading that chapter?

James 5:16 says that the effective prayer of a righteous person can accomplish much. Why is this kind of prayer so powerful?

How does someone become a righteous person?

CHAPTER TWENTY-ONE

Read John 16: 5-15. What did Jesus say the Holy Spirit will do for His disciples and for the world?

Based on this scripture, how have you seen the Spirit of God working in your life?

If God is the source of all joy, what does that tell you about His nature?

What will it be like to be in the presence of the Source of All Joy?

How much does God love each of us?

Why does God love us so much?

Describe the covenant that God the Father and Jesus Christ His Son has made with us.

What is God's purpose in this life for giving us gifts and blessings?

CHAPTER TWENTY-TWO

What is prayer?

How does God want His people to use prayer?

Why should we take praying seriously?

What happens when we pray?

What are some hindrances to our prayers? (*Isaiah 59:1-2; Matthew 6:14-15; James 1:6-7; I Peter 3:7*)

What do you think Paul meant when he said "*pray without ceasing,*" in I Thessalonians 5:16?

How important was prayer to Jesus while He was on the earth?

Are there things in your life that show that prayer is important to you?

CHAPTER TWENTY-THREE

Jesus said, "*No one can come to the Father unless the Father Who sent Me draws him.*" How did God draw you?

Based on this, when a person comes to God, who takes the first step?

With this information, describe some effective prayers we can offer on behalf of lost people.

Discuss what the Bible says about how a person receives salvation. (*Mark 16:16; Acts 2:38, 8:35-39,16:31, 22:16; Romans 10:9-10*)

CHAPTER TWENTY-FOUR

Why is unity among believers so important to Jesus?

What does it say to the world about God when His followers find ways to love each other?

What does it say to the world about God when His followers separate themselves from one another?

When bad things happen, why do we sometimes blame ourselves?

How may God use difficult and hard circumstances in our lives for our good?

How does God want us to respond when bad things happen?

Milton said that the most important thing Carol needed was Jesus. Do you agree or disagree? Explain your answer.

CHAPTER TWENTY-FIVE

Many people turn to drugs and alcohol to escape the pain of rejection, failure, or a miserable life. What is a better option?

What kind of help and support do people need who struggle with addictions?

How might Jesus want to provide that kind of support to others through you?

What does Jesus do in a person's life to change them from being selfish to being compassionate?

In II Peter 1:3-8 we are given insight and instruction on becoming '*partakers of the divine nature*'. What does that mean and how, according to these verses, does God accomplish that in us?

Why does God want people we meet to see His divine nature in us?

CHAPTER TWENTY-SIX

Describe what life is like without Jesus Christ.

What does hopelessness feel like?

The hope that Jesus offers can best be described as 'confident anticipation'. What does that kind of hope feel like?

Why must we be persistent and faithful in our prayers for others?

Describe some ways that we can use spiritual warfare in our service to Jesus.

It's easy to get distracted by thinking about all that Satan can do to oppose our work for Christ. What do you think the Hebrew writer had in mind when he tells us to *fix our eyes on Jesus*? (*Hebrews 12:2*)

How does following Jesus help us deal with the fear of what's on the other side of the veil?

Where does true joy and purpose in this life come from?

Appendix

About the Author

Alan W. Harris is a retired veterinarian who lives near Luray, Virginia, where he and Valerie, his wife of nearly fifty years, make their home. They have six children whom they homeschooled for twenty-seven years, a growing host of beautiful grandchildren, whom they adore,...and a pug.

Alan's motivation to write sprang from a desire to share an exciting story with his children. He wanted to not just entertain them, but to teach them important character and spiritual lessons. The tale needed to be very suspenseful, and the characters had to be engaging and fun in order to keep his children interested. The results were *The Tales of Larkin* series, which has five books. You can find out more about them as well as how to use them to teach at **StoriesChangeHearts.com**.

In searching for other subjects about which to write, Alan came up with *The Flintlock Sagas* series. which to date contains three books.

This new book, <u>The Other Side of the Veil</u>, is written more for adults and is meant not only to tell an interesting story, but also to challenge the reader to consider their everlasting future as well as God's will and His work in their lives on this side of the eternity. It is Alan's prayer that his new book, <u>The Other Side of the Veil</u>, will not only entertain his readers, but also help them grow in godly character and draw them closer to God the Father and His Son, King Jesus.

Other Works by Alan W. Harris
*(Find out more at **StoriesChangeHearts.com**)*

<u>*The Tales of Larkin*</u>

Book 1 **Hawthorn's Discovery** - <u>Hawthorn's Discovery</u> is a non-stop Christian adventure story of one inch tall woodland warriors. Full of fast-paced action, suspense and humor, this tale of deliverance is fun for the whole family.

Book 2 **Larkin's Journal** - This second book in the series is the prequel to book one and reveals the history of these tiny people. The story is of Larkin, son of Ramus, who will eventually become the patriarch of all of the Larkin tribes. From an early age Larkin's life is filled with adventure, danger, and intrigue; and he finds a loving Lord along the way.

Book 3 **The Great Gathering** - This story starts two years after Hawthorn and his friends in book one return from their secret exploits with the Makerian people. They are recruited to join a covert plan to bring the knowledge of the Maker's love to all the Larkin clans. The friends soon learn that following the King sometimes exacts a high cost. This book starts with a rush and continues with rapid-fire action and meaningful spiritual insights.

Book 4 **Mosstar and Belladonna** - This story takes place one hundred and fifty years in the Larkin's past. Not only must princess Belladonna and the tree laird's son survive frequent life-threatening dangers but they must face the Maker's truth about their own lives. Unknown to them is a diabolical plot to destroy them both and forever change the Larkin's future.

Book 5 **Fiery Trials** - This picks up the continuing story of Hawthorn and his friends. Two years have passed since the end of book three and the jealous Shaman have an opportunity to finally destroy the followers of Jehesus. Devastating disease and an unimaginable disaster must be faced if the King's followers are to survive.

The Flintlock Sagas

Book 1 **The Young Frontiersman** - Young William Hackett is a part of a group of pioneers starting a new life in the wilderness of Kentucky in the 1770's. They share constant peril, as well as facing the threat of attack by native warriors stirred up by British agents. Set during the Revolutionary War the exciting story demonstrates God's faithfulness to us, whether the battles we face are against physical enemies or spiritual ones.

Book 2 **The Maker's Medicine Girl** - No one knew the dangers of the Kentucky wilderness better than sixteen year old Remember Warren. Her village burned and her family and friends violently murdered by Indians, the girl found herself a slave of a renegade trapper and his Shawnee squaw. Though she doesn't believe it, God has not forsaken her. Will she look beyond the hardship and listen to God's higher purpose for all her suffering? The story reaches its climax as Ember is forced to make a desperate run for her life that will put her new faith to the extreme test.

Book 3 **The Dancing Ghosts** - Discovering the ghost-like figures dancing among the trees was enough to seriously concern Asa Whitlock and the two women with him. Then after the dancers tried to kill them as they raced back to Larkinboro, the town leaders knew they needed to know what was going on. Will Hackett, Grey Fox, Dirt Gurley, and Asa were sent to determine what these strange enemies were up to, but the more they learned the more terrifying the situation became. Eventually they must trust God and risk their lives to save their families, friends and even the American troops sent to defend them. Full of fast paced adventure, humor, and the faithfulness of God, this book will be hard to put down.

Keep up with Alan Harris, his short stories about the life of Jesus taken from the Gospel of John, *The Flintlock Sagas,* and his first series, *The Tales of Larkin,* as well as learning how to use stories to teach to the hearts of your children or students at **www.StoriesChangeHearts.com**.

If you wish to contact Alan you can e-mail him at **StoriesChangeHearts@gmail.com**.